Oliver P. Fuller

Historical Sketches of the Churches of Warwick

Rhode Island

Oliver P. Fuller

Historical Sketches of the Churches of Warwick
Rhode Island

ISBN/EAN: 9783337378844

Printed in Europe, USA, Canada, Australia, Japan

Cover: Foto ©Andreas Hilbeck / pixelio.de

More available books at **www.hansebooks.com**

HISTORICAL SKETCHES

OF THE

CHURCHES OF WARWICK,

RHODE ISLAND.

BY

OLIVER P. FULLER.

TO WHICH IS ADDED

A RECORD OF PERSONS JOINED IN MARRIAGE
IN THAT TOWN

BY

ELDER JOHN GORTON.

FROM

1754 TO 1792.

———— •✦• ————

PROVIDENCE
SIDNEY S. RIDER.
1880.

These sketches originally formed the appendix to the History of Warwick, Rhode Island, by the same author. The records of these societies date far back into the early history of the Colony, and are brought down to a very recent period. To this edition has been added the Record of persons joined in marriage by Elder JOHN GORTON, in the town of Warwick from 1754 to 1792. They are two hundred and eighty-one in number, and are of great value in tracing the genealogy of families living in Warwick and to some extent throughout the State.

HISTORICAL SKETCHES

OF THE

CHURCHES IN WARWICK, RHODE ISLAND.

INTRODUCTION.

The early ecclesiastical history of the town of Warwick is involved in much obscurity, and no reliable evidence exists of the formation of any independent church for about three-fourths of a century after the first settlement in 1642. That a respectable portion of the first settlers were Christian people there is no doubt. In 1639, John Greene, Richard Waterman, Francis Weston, Ezekiel Holliman, Wm. Arnold and Stukely Westcott, then residing in Providence, united with six others in church relation, and "agreed to support in faith and practice the principles of Christ's doctrine." These six men, whose names are above-mentioned, were among the earliest settlers of this town, three of them being among the original purchasers of the land. Before uniting in church relations at Providence, they had become "convinced of the truth of believers' baptism" by immersion, but had not had the privilege of practicing according to their faith. There was no minister of like sentiments, who had been immersed, to administer the ordinance of baptism, and to meet the difficulty they selected Ezekiel

Holliman, a " pious and gifted man," to baptize Roger Williams, which was accordingly done, when Mr. Williams in turn, baptized Mr. Holliman and the others. This was the origin of the First Baptist Church of Providence. Three years later, one-half the constituent members of that church settled within the limits of this town. There were others besides them who were professed Christians.*

Though it does not appear that there was an organ· ized church in the town for a considerable period, there are evidences that Holliman, Waterman and their associates who united in the formation of the church at Providence, still retained their membership in that body, visiting it as often as they found it convenient, but holding meetings of worship in their own town as a branch of the mother church. We have found no positive evidence of this, however. Rev. John Callender, then pastor of the First Baptist Church at Newport, in his famous centennial discourse, published in 1738, alluding to the First Church of Providence, says: " This church shot out into divers branches, as the members increased, and the distance of their habitation made it inconvenient for them to attend the public worship in town *Several meetings were fixed at different places,* and about the time the large township of Providence became divided into four towns,† these chapels of ease began to be considered as distinct churches, though all

---

* On March 13, 1639, at the General Court in Boston, "John Smith, for disturbing the public peace, by combining with others to hinder the orderly gathering of a church at Weymouth, and to set up another there, contrary to the orders here established, and the constant practice of all our churches, and for undue procuring the hands of many to a blank for that purpose, is fined £20, and committed during the pleasure of the Court or the Council."—*Mass Col. Rec. 1*, 252.

The name, John Smith, is a little confusing. Whether it was the same person of that name who became an early resident of this town, and was President of the Rhode Island Colony in 1649, I am not able to decide. After the above experience from the Massachusetts Court, he would have been likely to seek more hospitable regions. It is known that some of the Weymouth faction came to Rhode Island.

† This was in January, 1720-1.—*Arnold, Vol. II*, 102.

are yet in a union of counsels and interests."* On a
subsequent page, he says: "There are in the nine towns
on the main land, eight churches of the people, called
Baptists, one in every town except East Greenwich,
where there is, however, a Meeting House, in which
there is a meeting once a month.† In a note he adds
the names of Manasseh Martyn and Francis Bates as the
elders of the Warwick Church. Elder Martyn was ordained to the ministry in 1725, though the earliest records
of this church extant bear the date of 1741.‡

Allowing that the church here existed as a branch of
the First Church at Providence up to the time of the
division of the town of Providence, or about the
that time, the interval, during which we have no records
of a distinct church would be accounted for. If they
were only a branch church, their records would probably
be merged in those of the Providence Church.§ It is
well known that the doctrine of laying-on-of-hands, was

---

* Branch churches, with certain delegated powers from the mother
church, among which were the privileges of celebrating the communion and admitting members, have been common in Six Principle
churches from time immemorial. The membership of such
"Branches" was recorded with that of the parent church. See accounts of the Crompton Church and the Bethel of that order on subsequent pages.

† In 1730, says Backus, "there were thirteen Baptist churches,
most of them small, who held annual associations to promote disci-
pline and communion among them upon the six principles in Hebrews
VI."—Backus Hist. of the Baptists.

‡ Knight's History, p. 273.

§ On Friday, May 28, 1875, occurred the centennial anniversary of the
opening of the First Baptist Church of Providence, when an interesting and valuable address was delivered by Hon. Samuel G. Arnold.
From this address we make the following extract: "The church records begin in April, 1775, preceded by a list of members admitted from
December, 1774, during the great revival, to June 30, 1782. Prefixed
to the regular records, there is a 'History of the Baptist Church of
Christ in Providence, Rhode Island, being the oldest Baptist Church
in America,' with an introduction prepared in 1789, by John Stanford,
minister, then temporarily acting as pastor of the church. This is a
brief summary of such events as could then be collected respecting
the history of the church for a hundred and fifty years, from its foundation in 1639. Mr. Stanford's original manuscript of twenty folio
pages, is preserved in the archives of the Society, and has very
properly been copied into the first volume of the Church records. In

held by the First Church of Providence,* in a lax
manner at its beginning, but it " became afterwards a
term of communion, and continued so until after Dr.
Manning came among them; he prevailed with the
church to admit to *occasional* communion those brethren
who were not convinced of the duty of coming under
hands; but very few such were received as members till
after his death. On August 4, 1791, the church had a
full meeting, when this point was deliberately considered,
and a clear vote was gained to admit members who did
not hold that doctrine. But notwithstanding this vote,
the laying-on-of-hands, not as an ordinance, but as a
form of receiving new members, was generally practiced
until after the death of President Manning.† The first
church of Warwick was of the Six Principle order.

The alternative of supposing a branch church during
a period of three-fourths of a century as existing here,
would be that of supposing the strong personal influence
and peculiar religious opinions of Samuel Gorton, who
was a preacher, and sustained a religious meeting during
this time, prevented the formation of any church, or the
holding of any meetings that were not in accordance with
his views. At first we were inclined to this view. But
upon further research and consideration, the alternative
was rejected. That Mr. Gorton held a meeting during this
time is probable, but that the nucleus of the church,
which assumed an independent existence about the year
1725, had existed many years previous as a branch of
the First Church, Providence, seems worthy of credit.

Some account of Samuel Gorton and of his peculiar

1828, a small pamphlet was printed under the direction of the late
Nicholas Brown, then President of the Society, containing the charter
and by laws, together with the 'minutes of the early proceedings of
the Society from its first recorded meetings till 1793, when Dr. Gano
was called to the pastorate.' In this tract of sixteen pages, are preserved a complete transcript from the records for the first sixteen
months and the more important entries till the calling of Dr. Gano."

* Benedict's Hist. Vol. I, 487.

† Dr. Hague's Historical discourse, p. 107.

religious views, seem appropriate in this connection as
belonging to the ecclesiastical history of the town.
Though no church was formed in connection with his
ministrations, he exerted a powerful influence upon the
religious views of the colony. Benedict, in his history,
says: "Callender, Backus and others who have spoken of
Gorton's religious opinions, acknowledge that it is hard
to tell what he believed, but they assure us that it ought
to be believed that he held all the heresies that were
ascribed to him. The most we can learn is, that in alle-
gory and double-meanings of scripture he was similar to
Origen ; in mystical theology and the rejection of ordinances, he resembled the Quakers ; and the notion of
visible churches he utterly rejected." That he held all
the heresies that were ascribed to him, as intimated by
Dr. Benedict, is hardly to be credited, as some of them
that were published during the life of Gorton in " Morton's New England Memorial," were distinctly disa-
vowed by Gorton himself. The remark of Dr. Benedict
is too sweeping, and does not accord with the statement
of Callender, who says: "There are sufficient reasons why
we ought not and cannot believe he held all that are con-
fidently fathered upon him. For it is certain, that, whatever impious opinions his adversaries imputed to him, and
whatever horrid consequences they drew from the
opinions he owned, he ascribed as bad to them and fixed
as dreadful consequences upon their tenets ; and at the
same time in the most solemn manner, denies and disa-
vows many things they charge him with ; above all, when
he is charged with denying a future state and judg-
ment to come, both in theory and practice, he peremp-
torily and vehemently denies the charge, and solemnly
appeals to God and all that knew him, of the in-
tegrity of his heart and the purity of his hands ; and
avers that he always joins eternity with religion, as most
essential. And that the doctrine of the general salva-
tionists was the thing which his soul most hated.
[Answer to Morton's Memorial,—Calender, p. 92].
Calender further says: "He strenuously opposed the

doctrines of the people called Quakers. I am informed
that he and his followers maintained a religious meeting
on the first day of the week for above sixty years, and
that their worship consisted of prayers to God, of preaching, or expounding the scriptures and singing of psalms."
Dr. Benedict says: "He was a leader of a religious
meeting in Warwick above sixty years." This statement is incorrect, as he died in 1667, or twenty-five
years from the founding of the town. The statement of
Callender will come nearer to the truth "that he and his
followers" maintained a meeting for that length of time.
No church was organized by him or his followers, but
stated seasons of worship were held upon the Sabbath in
which the gospel was dispensed freely to all who would
listen to it. Among his chief heresies were the rejection
of an organized visible church and the ordinances connected with it; and from these peculiar views and those
of minor importance which grew out of them, sprang
most of the trouble between him and the other religious
sects. Morton in "New England's Memorial," gave a
summary of Gorton's religious opinions, which was published during Gorton's life. Gorton wrote to Mr.
Morton denying some of the charges made against him
in this book, especially that he had ever asserted that
there was "no state or condition after death," and says:
"I appeal to God, the judge of all secrets, that there
never was such a thought entertained in my heart." He
further says in answer to another charge: "we never
called sermons of salvation, tales; nor any ordinances of
the Lord, an abomination or vanity; nor holy ministers,
necromancers; we honor, reverence and practice these
things." In this letter he refers to a book published by
Mr. Winslow, which referred also to his sentiments, of
which Gorton says he had read but little, but was informed by Mr. Brown, who had been a commissioner for
the United Colonies, that "he would maintain that
there were forty lies published in that book." The letter may be found in the Appendix to Judge Staples'
edition of Simplicities' Defence.

Without attempting to state the religious views of Gorton with any degree of precision, it may perhaps be safely said that the essential gospel truths, as held by the great body of evangelical christians of the present day, were those that were held and preached by this somewhat singular man. That the difference that existed between his opinions, with the exception of those specially noted, and those of Williams and others, was rather imaginary than real, and grew out of the peculiar way in which he expresssd them, is evident. His published works are marvels of curious composition, with sentences so long and complicated, that it would make a school-master's blood run backwards, to analyze and parse them. Among these works the reader is referred to his "Incorruptible Key," printed in London, in 1647; "Saltmarsh returned from the Dead," printed in 1655; "Antidote against pharasaical Teachers," and "Antidote against the common Plague of the World;" "Simplicities Defence against a Seven Headed Church Policy," published in England, in 1646. These, with a manuscript commentary on the Lord's Prayer, of more than a hundred pages, now in possesion of the R. I. Historical Society, will furnish the curious reader with ample material for studying the religious tenets of the man. His "Simplicities Defence," is an historical narrative of the difficulties between the early settlers of this town and the colony of Massachusetts, growing out of the attempts of the latter to extend its jurisdiction over the lands and persons of the former. The account is written in his peculiar style, but is regarded as a fair account of the origin, progress, and issue of the unhappy controversy. Several valuable letters that passed between the parties during the time, are included in it, with much of a rambling theological character, in which the author delighted to indulge. The work is dedicated to the Earl of Warwick, whose friendly aid was received and duly acknowledged, and whom, as we have already stated, the settlers honored by giving his name to their town.*

Gorton was a man of acknowledged native talent, and with all his literary abstruseness and theological combativeness, exerted a large and for the most part a salutary influence in the community. When his opin-

---

* As a matter of curiosity, and as indicating Gorton's method of thought and style of composition, we give the following title pages to two of his works, his "Incorruptible Key," and his "Saltmarsh returned from the Dead."

"AN INCORRUPTIBLE KEY, composed of the CX Psalme wherewith you may open the Rest of the Holy Scriptures: Turning itself only according to the Composure and Art of that Lock, of the Closure and Science of that Great Mysterie of God manifest in the Flesh, but justified only by the Spirit which it evidently openeth and revealeth, out of Fall and Resurrection, Sin and Righteousness, Ascension and Descension, Height and Depth, First and Last, Beginning and Ending, Flesh and Spirit, Wisdom and Foolishness, Strength and Weakness. Mortality and Immortality, Jew and Gentile, Light and Darkness, Unity and Multiplication, Fruitfulness and Barrenness, Care and Blessing, Man and Woman, All Suffering and Deficiency, God and Man. And out of every unity made up of twaine, it openeth that great two-leafed Gate which is the sole Entrie into the city of God of New Jerusalem, _into which none but the king of Glory can enter:_ and as the Porter openeth the doore of the Sheepfold, by which whosoever entereth in, is the Shepherd of the Sheep: See Isa. 45, 1; Psal. 24, 7, 8, 9, 10: John 10, 1, 2, 3; Or, (according to the signification of the word translated Psalme) it is a pruning knife, to lop off from the church of Christ all superfluous Twigs of earthly and carnal commandments. Levitical services or Ministry and fading and vanishing Priests or Ministers, who are confirmed by Death as holding no correspondency with the princely Dignity, Office and Ministry of an Melchisedek who is the only Ministry of the Sanctuary and of that true Tabernacle which the Lord pitcht and not Man. For it supplants the Old Man and implants the new: abrogates the Old Testament or Covenant and confirms the New into a thousand generations, or in generations forever. By Samuel Gorton, Gent. and at the time of penning hereof, in the place of Judicature (upon Aquethneck alias Road Island) of Providence Plantations in the Nanhygansett Bay, New England. Printed in the yeere 1647."

"SALTMARSH RETURNED FROM THE DEAD, in _Amicus Philalethes:_ or the Resurrection of James the Apostle out of the Grave of Carnal Glosses for the correction of the universal Apostacy which cruelly burried him who yet liveth. Appearing in the Comely Ornaments of his Fifth Chapter in an exercise, June 5, 1654. Having laid by his grave clothes in a despised village remote from England, but wishing well and heartily desiring the True Prosperity thereof."—_Mackie's Life of Gorton in Spark's Am. Biog._

That such language may have been perfectly intelligible to Gorton himself, we have no disposition to doubt; that it may have conveyed more to his contemporaries who were acquainted with the circumstances that called it forth, and had become familiar with such forms of expression, than to us, may be true. That it lacks a little of that perspicuity, which in modern times is regarded as an excellence in writing or speaking, is quite evident.

ions on civil or religious topics were opposed, he showed much of that quality that might be termed, " otherwise-mindedness," and, at times, exhibited a " superfluity of naughtiness," but otherwise was of a generous and sympathetic nature, and inclined to award to others the same liberty of thought and expression which he claimed for himself.

We close this account of him with an extract taken from the manuscript Itinerary of Dr. Styles, a former clergyman of Newport, and afterwards President of Yale College, as given by Judge Staples :

"At Providence, Nov. 18, 1771, I visited aged Mr. John Angell, ae. 80, born, Oct. 18, 1691, a plain, blunt-spoken man; right old English frankness. He is not a Quaker, nor Baptist, nor a Presbyterian, but a Gortonist, and the only one I have seen. Gorton now lives in him, his only disciple left. He says he knows of no other and that he is alone. He gave me an account of Gorton's disciples, first and last, and showed me some of Gorton's printed books and some of his manuscripts. He said Gorton wrote in heaven and no one can understand his writings, but those who live in heaven while on earth. He said that Gorton had beat down all outward ordinances of Baptism and the Lord's Supper with unanswer-able demonstrations. That Gorton preached in London in Oliver's time, and had a church and living of £500 a year offered him, but he believed no sum would have tempted him to take a farthing for preaching. He told me that his grandfather, Thomas Angell, came from Salem to Providence with Roger Williams, that Gorton did not agree with Roger Williams, who was for outward ordinances set up by new apostles. I asked if Gorton was a Quaker; as he seemed to agree with them in rejecting outward ordinances. He said no; and that when George Fox (I think) or one of the first Friends came over; he went to Warwick to see Gorton, but was a mere babe to Gorton. The Friends had come out of the world some ways, but still were in darkness or twilight, but that Gorton was far beyond them, he said, high way up to the dispensation of light. The Quakers were in no way to be com-pared with him; nor any man else can, since the primitive times of the church, especially since they came out of Popish darkness. He said Gorton was a holy man; wept day and night for the sins and blindness of the world; his eyes were a fountain of tears, and always full of tears—a man full of thought and study—had a long walk out through the trees or woods by his house, where he constantly walked morning and evening, and even in the depth of the night, alone by himself, for contemplation and the enjoyment of the dispensation of light. He was universally beloved by all his neighbors and the Indians, who esteemed him not only as a friend, but one high in communion with God in heaven, and indeed he lived in heaven.''

In preparing the following accounts of the churches, the author communicated with the pastors or some leading members of the several churches now existing in the town, inviting them to furnish a brief sketch of their respective churches, for publication. In several instances the invitation was accepted, and in others the records of the churches were kindly placed in his hands to enable him to furnish the accounts. He regrets that in a few instances, either from a loss of the records or lack of interest in the subject, on the part of those to whom he applied, he has failed to receive the desired information concerning several. Where the accounts have been prepared by others, due acknowledgement has been given. In the other cases, where church records have been kindly placed in his hands from which to make up the accounts, such accounts have received, in each case, the approval of some one or more of the leading members of the church, to whom they were submitted before publishing:

OLD BAPTIST CHURCH, OLD WARWICK.*

This church, which has had for the past thirty years merely a nominal existence, is the oldest one in the town, having probably existed as a branch of the First Baptist Church of Providence, nearly or quite a half century before it assumed an independent existence. The earliest records of the church bear the date of 1741, though the origin of the body as a distinct and independent church, must have been as early as 1725. Backus' history mentions it in 1730 as then existing. Previous

---

* The six principles, or doctrines, held by this church may be found in Hebrews VI., 1, 2.

to that date, and reaching back to about the time of the first settlement of the town, it probably existed as a branch of the First Baptist Church of Providence, of which several of the original settlers of the town were constituent members. Hence the history of the body previous to the organization as a separate church would be incorporated with that of the First church of Providence. As there are no original records of this latter church extant, previous to April, 1775, it is impossible to determine the exact status of the body previous to that date. In 1730, the church at Old Warwick consisted of 65 members, under the pastoral care of Elder Manasseh Martin.* Elder Martin having served the church as pastor upwards of 30 years, died March 20th, 1754. He lies buried in the cemetery near the site of the Meeting House where he preached. A heavy slab half embedded in the earth, with his name and date of death, marks the spot. His widow, who afterwards be-
c the wife of Elder Charles Holden, lies beside him.

On the 18th of June, 1744, Chr ammett was ordained as colleague of Mr. Martin, and seems to have extended his labors beyond the immediate precincts of Old Warwick, gathering many into the church from remote regions. He served the old church " upwards of six years," according to the inscription upon his tombstone, dying in the 48th year of his age. He lies buried also, in the yard of the old meeting-house.

On June 16, 1757, Charles Holden was ordained pastor of the church, and continued to preach until old age and its infirmities compelled him to relinquish his post. He was ordained in the 62d year of his age, and died June 20th, 1785, in his ninetieth year. He lies buried in a quiet spot, some thirty or forty rods west of the residence of John Wickes Greene, Esq. Elder Holden had a son and also a grandson named Charles. Among

---

* See "The History of the General or Six Principle Baptists in Europe and America," by Elder Richard Knight, published in 1827. Elder Knight was the esteemed and useful pastor of the Scituate church.

his lineal descendants was the late John Holden, of Crompton, father of the late Thomas R. Holden, of Providence. Previous to the declaration of American Independence, it was customary for ministers, following the old English custom, to pray for the king in their public worship. One Sabbath after the Declaration, while the Elder was praying, forgetting for the moment the change that had taken place in the political condition of the country, he reached the place where the usual petition for the king came in, and before he was aware he uttered it—" we pray for the king and all in authority "—when suddenly checking himself and hesitating he added with emphasis—*"living in Rhode Island!"* The limiting clause of the petition thus forcibly expressed, established his patriotism. In his will, Elder Holden made provision for the liberation of his several slaves. Dimmis was to have her freedom on the decease of her master, and her youngest son was given her until the age of twenty one, when he was to be free. His slave Dinah was to be set at liberty at eighteen years of age, and Prince, Cato and Morocco, when they reached the age of twenty-one, provided they behaved properly up to those ages. A small bequest was made to each of them in addition to their freedom.

Benjamin Sheldon was ordained assistant to Elder Holden, June 18, 1778, by Elders Holden, J. Wightman, John Gorton and Reuben Hopkins. October 10, 1782, Abraham Lippitt was ordained as an assistant elder in this church, by Elders Nathan Peirce, John Gorton* and J. Wightman. About the year 1793, Elder Lippitt removed to the West, and the following year the church called Samuel Littlefield to the pastoral

---

* Elder John Gorton was the pastor of the church at East Greenwich, for many years, and preached in a meeting house that stood not far from the shore, but which has been demolished many years. He was a descendant of Samuel Gorton, one of the first settlers of the town, and the great-grandfather of Mrs. Wm. B. Spencer of Phenix. He officiated at the marriage of General Nathaniel Greene. An old book before me, owned by Mr. Henry W. Greene, the leaves of which

office, and he was ordained February 17, 1794. He continued to preach until about 1825, when he had a paralytic shock which laid him aside from active life.

The old meeting-house, a sketch of which is given in the engraving, was built by this church at an early date, and is probably the earliest one built in this town of which any knowledge at present exists. It was taken down in the spring of 1830. It was in a very decayed

THE OLD MEETING HOUSE, OLD WARWICK.

(From a pencil sketch by Mrs. C. W. Colgrove.)

condition when demolished. Its size was about forty feet square, with two doors, one on the side facing the Conimicut road, a double door, and one fronting Meet-

---

are partly of the "Stamp" paper of the times, and bound in sheep skin, with a brazen clasp, contains the records of 281 marriages, in Elder Gorton's writing. The first marriage, that of Anthony Low and Phebe Greene, bears the date of January 1, 1754, the last, that of George Finney and Hanahretty Matthews, daughter of Caleb Matthews, May 4, 1792. The Warwick and Coventry Baptist Church was organized at the house of Caleb Matthews, October 21, 1805.

ing-House road, so called.   In the rear was a burying
ground, owned by the Low family.   The building was
without bell or steeple.   Its internal arrangements were
peculiar : the platform for the preacher was raised some
two or three feet, with a small desk for the Bible to rest
upon, and in the rear were seats for the preacher, the
deacon and the constable.   The deacon usually lined oft
the hymns for the singers.   There were three large
square pews in front of the platform, and their occupants
were supposed to be entitled to special respect.   Other
pews ranged along the sides of the building, with one
long pew for the deacon's family.   The seats for the
congregation generally, were rude benches.   There were
galleries on two sides of the house with stairways leading up to them from the audience room.   The whole in-
terior was open to the roof.   Before the old house was
given up, it had become so dilapidated, that the case of
the Hebrew sanctuary mentioned by David in the
eighty-fourth psalm was repeated—" the sparrow hath
found a house and the swallow a nest for herself, where
she may lay her young, even thine altars, O Lord of
Hosts "—and meetings were held in the school-house.
A farewell service was held in it October 4, 1829, and is
still remembered by some who were present, and from
whom the writer has received these items.*   Elder Wm.
Manchester on that day baptized, at a place called the
" new bridge," Mary Almira and Louisa Waterman.
It was sold soon after, and a portion of the materials
worked up into the dwelling-house that now stands
nearly opposite the residence of John Holden, Esq.

Their new house, the one now occupied by the Shawo-
met Baptist Church, was dedicated in 1829, Elder Wm.
C. Manchester preaching the sermon, from Gen. xxviii. 17.
The pastor at the time was Elder Job Manchester, who
had been ordained October, 1828.   He was from Coventry, and had married a daughter of the late Thomas Staf-

---

* John Wickes Greene, Esq., a former member and clerk of the old
church, and others.

ford, one of their leading members. He is said to have been an able minister, and by his liberal and enlightened views prepared the way for the future enlargement of the church. An extensive revival was enjoyed during the year 1829, in which twenty-two persons united with the church. In 1843 he resigned his charge and removed to Providence, where he united with the Stewart Street Baptist Church. He died August 9th, 1859, aged 75.* In 1830, in a letter to the " General Meeting," they reported fifty-four members. Their prospects from this time began to wane, their members were gradually reduced by death and dismission, until dependent upon occasional supplies in preaching, they became disheartened and finally gave up their meetings. They have had only a nominal existence for many years. Mr. Daniel Arnold, of Crompton, who died last year, left legacies to this church, and to those at Crompton and Birch Hill, which has brought to light the existence of a few members, who claim to be the church; their names are Benoni Lockwood, Aurelia Weaver, Lucy A. Lockwood, and Eliza T. Lockwood.

As there was some doubt existing as to the ownership of the land upon which the house was built, the town, at a meeting held April 15, 1829, made the following provision, viz. : .

" Whereas certain public spirit Individuals in the Town of Warwick, have it in contemplation to erect a Meeting House for the worship of Almighty God, in that Section of the Town usually called Old Warwick, and on Land near the school house which Land is represented to have been originally reserved by the proprietors for the purpose of Education and as a tanning field; and doubts have arisen Whether the Town may not possess an Interest in said Land either by Escheat or some other title, Now therefore with the intention of promoting a project so Laudable by perfecting the title of the Individuals aforesaid

---

* Elder Job Manchester was a skillful mechanic as well as an able pastor and preacher. As early as 1816 he invented a power loom, for weaving cotton cloth, and in 1818 made some improvements on the Bed Tick or Twilled work, looms. He was a practical machinist. *See Transactions of the R. I. Society for the Encouragement of Domestic Industry for 1861, pp. 61-76.*

" It is voted, That it shall be the duty of the Treasurer of the Town whenever a Meeting House aforesaid shall have been erected to Release on the part of the Town all Right and Title to that part of the Lot whereon it may be placed. It being understood that the same is to Include a piece of Ground Eight rods square."

OLD BAPTIST CHURCH AT APPONAUG.

At a church meeting held at Old Warwick, of which Elder Manasseh Martin was pastor, Dec. 6, 1744, Benjamin Peirce and wife, Ezrikham Peirce and wife, Edward Case and wife, John Budlong, and such others as wished to form a church at the Fulling Mill, of the same faith and order, were granted leave. Several members from East Greenwich united with them, and the church was duly organized. Benjamin Peirce was ordained their minister. They eventually erected a meeting house, " on an eminence East of the village of Apponaug which commanded an extensive prospect of this village, river, islands and surrounding country." It stood nearly opposite of the present residence of C. R. Hill, Esq. There is a tradition that it was built at the suggestion of Elder Peter Worden, who in 1758-9 had built a house of worship in Coventry, " 28 feet long by 26 feet wide and two stories high," and preached in it many years and afterwards settled in Apponaug. It is said that this house was of the same dimensions as the one in Coventry which became known in later times as the Elder Charles Stone meeting house, Elder Stone having been the successor of Elder Worden. Mr. Worden was born near Westerly, June 6, 1728, and is represented as a man of large stature, with a powerful voice, and a useful rather than a very intellectual man. After leaving Apponaug, he removed to Cheshire, Mass., in 1770, where another edition of " 28 by 26" without revisal or improvement was erected, and where he continued to hold forth the word of life. He died in 1808, in his 80th year. He preached in Coventry and Warwick nineteen years.

The church became involved in difficulty owing to some change in the religious sentiments of Elder Pierce, and diminished in members and was finally dissolved, and " their meeting house went to decay for many years." At what precise period this occurred does not appear, but it was previous to the revolutionary war.

Elder Knight, in his history, makes no mention of any other pastor than Elder Peirce, in connection with this church, and it is probable that the connection of Elder Worden was of short duration. Of the subsequent history of Elder Peirce the writer has no knowledge. The Peirces furnished a number of Elders to the church in different places. Elder Nathan Peirce was settled over the Rehoboth church many years, and till his death in 1794. Elders Preserved Peirce and Philip Peirce, brothers, were ordained in the same church about the year 1800. The latter soon after removed west.

Soon after the close of the revolutionary war another church was organized. The date of the organization is given by Elder Knight in one part of his work as 1785, and in another as 1792. As we have had no access to the original records we are unable to settle the point. David Corpe, a member of the East Greenwich church, from which the new one was set off, was ordained their pastor. They occupied the old house, which was repaired and made comfortable. Elder Corpe, becoming advanced in years and reduced in pecuniary means, resigned his trust and removed to an estate which he held in the northwest part of the State. Elder Spooner was his successor, having been appointed by the yearly meeting to supply them with preaching once a month. The tide of prosperity turned against them, and in 1805 the church followed the example of its predecessor and became extinct.

The old meeting house, after resounding with the messages of the Gospel for many years, finally lost its identity more than fifty years ago, and a portion of it may be found in a private residence a few rods north of the spot where it originally stood. There are a few persons now

*3

living who remember it, as the place where in their childhood they were accustomed to assemble on the Sabbath and listen to the lengthy discourses of the early preachers.

THE BETHEL SIX PRINCIPLE BAPTIST CHURCH.

This church is a grandchild of the Old Warwick Church. The Coventry or "Maple Root" Church * was set off from the latter church, May 17, 1744, though the latter church does not appear to have been formally organized until Oct. 14, 1762. The church for many years and until 1857, was known as the Phenix Branch of the Maple Root Church. While sustaining this relation to the Maple Root, worship was conducted in the Arkwright school house and the private houses in Phenix, until the school house was built in the latter place in 1827, when the building was used one Sabbath per month until the church built a meeting house. Elder Thomas Tillinghast preached many years in the old Arkwright school house, and when the Phenix school house was built, divided a monthly Sabbath between the two school houses. In 1838, they built a meeting house in Phenix, which was the second house built in that village for exclusive religious purposes. The building committee were Dea. Johnson, Wm. C. Ames and Robert Levalley. The house was built by John R. Brayton, now of Knightsville, who built the Tatem Meeting House previously. The house was about sixty feet long, thirty-six wide, with eighteen feet posts, and is said to have cost about $3,000. This was a large sum in those days, and, as it proved, a larger one than the church was able to pay, and the debt incurred resulted in disaster to the church. After struggling along for many

---

* This church is usually, now, called the "Maple Root Church." Elder Knight, the historian of the denomination, calls it the "Maypole" Root Church, and I am informed by Dea. Andrews, it is so designated in the earliest records of the church.

years the church became somewhat divided and weakened, and their house was sold at public auction to Dr. McGreggor for $1,000, who afterwards sold it to Cyrus Manchester for $1,100. On Sept. 25, 1851, it was again sold to Wm. B. Spencer, Esq., who finally converted it into tenements, for which purpose it is still used.

The last pastor of the Phenix Branch Church was Elder Stephen Thomas, whose denominational sentiments underwent some change, and in the year 1851, he closed his labors, and subsequently became pastor of the present Baptist Church at Natick. Elder Thomas afterwards became pastor at Holme's Hole, now called Vineyard Haven, where he died a few years ago. The church was now houseless and pastorless, and continued in an un· settled condition until it gathered up its little remaining strength about the year 1857, and made arrangements for the building of a new house of worship at Birch Hill.

In June, 1857, a petition signed by ninety-four persons, members of the "Maple Root" Church in Coventry, setting forth that they had "for a long time been known as the Phenix Branch of said Coventry Church," and had now erected a house of worship at Birch Hill, was presented to the said Maple Root Church, praying that they might be organized into a separate and independent body. Among the petitioners were Elders Benjamin B. Cottrell, Henry B. Locke and Nathaniel W. Warren. On the third of the following month the petition was granted, and on the twenty-sixth of that month, they were duly organized as a distinct church. Elder Thomas Tillinghast, preached, Ephesians II, 19, 20, 21. Elders B. B. Cottrell, H. B. Locke and N. W. Warner participated in the exercises. At this point the records, which have been very well kept by the several clerks, begin.

On Saturday, August 22, 1857, Elder Thomas Tillinghast, was chosen pastor, and Wanton A. Whitford, clerk. On Oct. 31, 1858, "Elder B. B. Cottrell, Dea. Benjamin Essex and W. A. Whitford were appointed trustees to receive and hold in trust a deed of a lot of land on Birch Hill in Warwick, appropriated for a meeting house for said church and denomination." The house was regarded by some as too small, and at a meeting held Jan. 9, 1859, a proposition was made to enlarge the "Bethel," by an addition of twelve feet to its length, and Dea. Essex, Henry Remington and W. A. Whitford, were appointed a committee to make the alterations. The funds for making the proposed addition did not seem to be forthcoming, and the committee hesitated to commence the work of building under the circumstances, and on the following October were instructed to make the addition "forthwith," on the front of the house. The addition was accordingly made and a debt incurred, which became a serious obstacle to the prosperity of the church. The building had to be mortgaged, and was in danger of following in the steps of the previous house at Phenix. Failing to obtain funds by subscription, the money was subsequently raised by festivals held about ten years ago under the direction of Mrs. Bowen A. Sweet, one of the members, the amount of $675 being raised, more than sufficient to clear the house of debt.

Previous to the year 1860, the covenant meetings were held at Arkwright every other month, and the communion monthly at the Bethel, subsequently it was voted to hold the communion services once in three months at Arkwright. On March 25, 1860, Wanton A. Whitford, was ordained as a deacon. Previous to the ordination the candidate was questioned as to his religious views, and also his views on the subjects of Temperance and Slavery. "The wife of the candidate was then called upon to express her mind in regard to her becoming a Deacon's wife, when she arose and expressed a willingness to do her duty in that respect." April 28, 1861, Henry Remington, a member of the church, was ordained to the gospel ministry, and afterwards became assistant pastor. April 16, 1864, Bowen A. Sweet was elected church clerk, in which position he has continued to the present time.

At a covenant meeting held August 28, 1864, a letter

was sent to the Association, in which it is stated that
they had had no pastor since the death of Elder Thomas
Tillinghast, that the church had been passing through
severe trials, and giving as their statistics the following:
Dismissed by letter, 4 ; excluded, 4; dropped, 4 ; dead,
1; Total, 138. Oct. 23, 1864, Elder Samuel Arnold
was unanimously elected pastor, and accepted the
position.

At a meeting held Jan. 26, 1868, Elder Arnold, upon
petition of several members of the Bethel Church, residing in Swansey, read the following resolution, which
was adopted : "Voted and resolved, that the Brethren
and Sisters of this church, residing in the State of Massachusetts, be set off as a branch of the same, to be
called the Swansey Branch, together with such others as
shall become associated with them, with the privilege of
receiving and dismissing members and holding communion." Number of members in September, 1874, 115.

Elder Samuel Arnold still continues the pastor of the
church, though living in Providence, and preaching at
the Bethel but once a month. Elder Nathaniel W.
Warner lived at Natick, where he died August 6th,
1858. Elder Henry B. Locke died November 10, 1865.
Elder B. B. Cottrell, also one of the constituent members of this church, is at present the acceptable pastor of
the Tabernacle Church in Fiskeville. By his efforts a
Meeting House was built at a cost of about $1,700,'
which was dedicated July 24th, 1873, and a church
soon after organized. Dea. Benjamin Essex, who has
resided in the vicinity for the past twenty-six years, and
is also one of the constituent members of the church,
still serves the church as deacon, and continues as prompt
and punctual in his religious duties, as the " Regulator "
that hangs in his workshop, and ticks away the time in
measured beats from year to year. The late Daniel
Arnold, of Crompton, bequeathed to this church a portion of his personal property, but the exact amount the
church will receive is not at present known.

CROMPTON SIX PRINCIPLE BAPTIST CHURCH.

In the winter of 1841, six persons who subsequently united with others in the formation of this church, commenced holding meetings in the old Centreville schoolhouse. Their meetings were interesting, and a revival soon followed, which resulted in the conversion of about thirty persons who were baptized most of them into the fellowship of the Maple Root church, in Coventry. Elder Henry B. Locke had come from the southern part of the State and united with the Maple Root Church, and seems to have been a successful laborer with this little band of brethren. Before the middle of April he baptized the thirty converts, who united with the Maple Root church. April 23, 1842, a petition was presented to the Maple Root church, signed by thirty eight persons, praying to be set off as a Branch Church. The prayer was granted, and Elder H. B. Locke was chosen pastor, C. A. Carpenter, deacon and William Rice, clerk. Elder Locke remained the pastor until November 1843, and was followed by Elder William P. Place, who continued in office until April 19, 1857, and then removed to Pennsylvania, remaining there about a year and then returned to Rhode Island.

Soon after the brethren were set off from the mother church in Coventry as a branch, they united their efforts to secure a permanent place for worship. Mrs. Sarah Remington, widow of James E. Remington, gave them a lot of land consisting of about a quarter of an acre, on certain conditions, among which were, that the church should build a meeting-house upon it within six months, keep it in good repair and use it, or allow it to be used only for religious purposes, failing in which, the lot was to revert to the grantor, her heirs, assigns, &c. The deed, which is dated December 26, 1843, further provided "that said house shall be open and free for all religious societies, when not occupied by said branch of

the Crompton Mills Six Principle Baptist Society."
The house was dedicated September 7th, 1844. The
church continued as a branch of the Maple Root, until
April 10, 1845, when it was formally organized as an
independent church. On September 6, 1845, it united
with the yearly Conference. November 28, 1850,
William Rice was ordained as a deacon.

At the conclusion of Elder Place's labors, Elder Locke
was recalled to the pastorate, and remained two years,
when he died. Elder Wilcox preached two Sabbaths a
month, for several years and until his last sickness. In
the spring of 1868, Elder Ellery Kenyon became pastor,
and continued until January 15, 1871, when he resigned.
Sunday May 15, 1870, Wm. R. Johnson was baptized,
and on the same day was ordained to the ministry, the
ordination services being conducted by Elders Kenyon,
Arnold and Wilcox. On March 23, 1871, the church
unanimously elected Elder Wm. R. Johnson as its pastor and he continued thus until the present year. The
church at present is without a pastor, though enjoying
the preaching of Elder Slocum.

William Rice, C. A. Carpenter, C. M. Seckell and
William Price have served the church as deacons;
William Rice, E. W. Sweet, John Wood, Sheldon H.
Tillinghast, Wm. P. Place, as clerks. The present clerk,
is Eben W. Sweet. The late Daniel Arnold bequeathed
to this church a portion of his personal property, the
exact amount of which, has not yet been determined.

CONGREGATIONAL CHURCH, RIVER POINT.

On the 7th of February, 1849, an ecclesiastical
council convened at the meeting-house, at River
Point, for the purpose of organizing an Evangelical Congregational Church. After the usual preliminaries, the
council voted unanimously in favor of the project, and
organized the following persons as a church, viz.: John
L. Smith, Jeremiah K. Aldrich, Brigham C. Deane,

Mary Greene, Phila B. Deane, Priscilla G. Seagraves, Hannah L. Sweet, Lucy Hill, Hannah Hall and Susan E. Smith

Rev. George Uhler at the time of the organization of the church, appears to have been preaching in the place, and was engaged by the church as its "stated supply," although he is spoken of in subsequent records as the pastor of the church. He continued his labors until ill health induced him to relinquish his position, June 12, 1853. On the following June 13th, a call was extended to Rev. S. B. Goodenow, at a salary of $700, which was accepted, and Mr. Goodenow entered upon his work the first Sabbath in December 1853 ,and remained until June 5, 1855, when he resigned and went to Ulster, N. Y. From this time, the church having become somewhat weakened by loss of quite a number of its members, was without regular pastoral labor until 1857, with the exception of about nine months in 1856, when Rev. Mr. Woodbury officiated as a supply.

Rev. George W. Adams was installed pastor of the church, September 30, 1857, and died after a somewhat prolonged sickness, December 9, 1862. Mr. Adams was a sound theologian and an excellent pastor, and was beloved by the church and community. He was a diligent student and prepared his sermons with much care. We remember hearing him say that he had sixty fully written sermons that he had never preached. His death most deeply afflicted his family. Rev. Mr. Williams, who had been supplying the church during the pastor's illness, continued to preach until February, when several of the pastors connected with the Rhode Island Congregational Association kindly volunteered their services in supplying the pulpit until the last Sabbath in April, in order that the salary of the deceased pastor might be continued to his bereaved family.

On Feb. 6, 1864, the church by an unanimous invitation engaged the Rev. J. K. Aldrich to supply the pulpit the following year. This arrangement continued until August, 1867, when Mr. Aldrich removed to East

Bridgewater, Mass., to assume the pastoral care of the Union Congregational Church in that place. Mr. Aldrich was during this time, as for several years previously, also, Principal of an English and Classical School in the vicinity. He was followed by Rev. Lyman H. Blake, who received a call from the church Oct. 6, 1867, and was ordained and installed as pastor on Nov. 14th, following. Mr. Blake continued the pastor until Oct. 3, 1869, when he resigned to assume a pastorate at Rowley, Mass. Since then the church has been without a settled pastor, though enjoying during most of the time the ministrations of the word from various ministers, as "stated," or occasional supplies. Like nearly all churches it has had its seasons of adversity as well as of prosperity. One hundred and twenty-five persons have had their names enrolled upon its list of membership, sixty-two of whom were received on their confession of faith in the Redeemer, and the remainder by letters. Ten have died while members, two were excommunicated, and fifty-eight dismissed to unite with other churches, leaving the present number (April, 1875) fifty-five. John L. Smith and Henry Harris have served the church as deacons, and Jeremiah K. Adams, George T. Arnold and Thomas M. Holden as clerks. The records of this church have been unusually well kept, some of its clerks not only recording the ordinary business of the church, but also the births, marriages and deaths of those connected with it.

THE WARWICK AND COVENTRY BAPTIST CHURCH.*

The house of worship connected with this church is located in the village of Crompton. The legal title of the society, which is composed of such persons as are elected from the male members of the church, none others being eligible, is, The First Baptist Society of

---

* The account of this church is from a recent discourse of the pastor, in commemoration of the seventieth anniversary of its organization.

4

Warwick. The society possesses and controls the church property. The church is one of the mother churches of the town, having formerly embraced within her parish boundaries the territory now shared by about a score of churches of various orders which she has seen spring up around her. For this reason a somewhat extended account of her origin and progress may perhaps be allowed.

Three periods may be noticed. The first, extending from the organization to the building of the "Tin Top" meeting-house in Quidnick, in 1808; the second, from that event to the building of the meeting-house in Crompton, in 1843; and the third, from that year to the present time.

The first period embraces only about two and a half years of time, and was of an unsettled, migratory character, in which the church wandered about from place to place seeking for a permanent home. It commenced October 21, 1805, on which date a number of converts belonging to East Greenwich, Warwick and North Kingstown, met at East Greenwich, at the house of Mr. Caleb Mathews, and after due consideration, decided " to unite together under the name of the United Brethren and Sisters of East Greenwich, Warwick and North Kingstown." On the 11th of November following, a council consisting of delegates from the First and the Second Baptist Churches of Providence, the one at Rehoboth and the one at North Kingstown, assembled, and after the usual examinations, recognized them as a Christian church, with the title of " The Baptist Church of East Greenwich, Warwick and North Kingstown." Thirty-seven persons, nine of whom were men, composed the organization. With the exception of Deacon Shaw and his wife, who were received by letter from the First Church, Providence, they appear to have been at the time but recently converted. Asa Niles, an unordained brother, had been preaching in East Greenwich and Centreville, and revival blessings had followed his earnest labors. Quite a number of persons had been converted, who afterwards united in the formation of this church.

Though Mr. Niles did not join the new church, and was not formally recognized as its pastor, he continued to preach for it until the May following, when the care of the church was given to Rev. David Curtis.

Rev. Asa Niles was born in Braintree, Mass., Feb. 10, 1777. While in business in Boston, he attended Dr. Baldwin's church and was converted. Being convinced of his duty to preach the gospel, he gave up his business and moved to Beverly, where he studied with "Father Williams." Rev. Mr. Williams had several students at the time. Having finished his studies, he came into Rhode Island as a missionary, and labored at Paw-tucket, Pawtuxet, East Greenwich and Centreville. He was an earnest, pointed preacher, and the truths that he uttered awakened much opposition among "the baser sort," some of whom in the villages of Pawtuxet and East Greenwich threatened him with personal violence. At one time, while he was preaching, one of this class threw a stone at him through a window, which passed by his head, striking a woman and breaking her arm. Elder Niles kept the stone for about twenty-five years. At another time they took his horse, on which he rode to his appointments, and sheared his mane and tail, but it does not appear that he preached any less faithfully on account of these persecutions. After leaving this church, he preached in Middletown, Conn., four years; Windsor, Vt., four years; Salem, Mass., six years; Scituate. Mass., Weare, N. H., Haver-hill, Mass., and then went to Middleboro, Mass., where he died April 16, 1849, at the age of 72 years. His mind became impaired at the age of sixty-five, and there was a gradual decay of his mental powers until he died. At his funeral there were six of his fellow ministers, who bore grateful testimony to his worth as a servant of Christ.

The church worshipped at East Greenwich a portion of the time in the Court House and also in an old meeting-house that has since been destroyed. At Centreville they worshipped in the school-house, in the building now used by Mr. Gould as a wheelwright's shop. This building had been erected for both school and religious purposes and, was solemnly dedicated to God with appropriate services. The Methodists also used it a part of the time. It was furnished with a gallery for the singers over the entrance, and is remembered gratefully by the few remaining individuals who were interested worshippers at the time. The larger portion of the church residing in the region of Centreville, it was finally

decided to erect a suitable sanctuary where they would
be better accommodated, and Quidnick being a central
position, was chosen as the place. In view of this the
church voted on the 27th of February, 1808, to change
its name to the Baptist Church of Warwick and Coventry,
which it still retains. This closes the first period of its
history.

The first event of importance in the second period is
the erection of the new meeting-house, which soon
became widely known as the " Tin Top," so called from
the steeple or cupola being covered with tin. Its dimensions were sixty feet long by forty wide, with a commo-
dious vestry. Its galleries extended around three sides
of the building. The building was framed in Providence, and rafted down the river and around to Apponaug, and thence drawn by teams to the place of erection. It is said to have been raised and completed in
two months, and cost $3,300. The land on which it
stands was given by Mr. Jacob Greene. Probably no
building ever erected in Kent County ever awakened so
much interest as this. People living miles away, with
curiosity excited, came and viewed it with wondering
delight. Boys from the neighboring villages ran away
from school, attracted by its glittering tower. Large
congregations gathered for worship within its walls, and
the church, with grateful pride, viewed the result of
their toils and sacrifices. They had assumed, however,
more pecuniary responsibility than they felt able to bear,
and, in accordance with the custom of the times, they
applied for and received of the General Assembly permission to raise $2,000 by a lottery. (Similar grants
had been made to other churches. One to St. John's
Church, Providence, in March 23, 1762, for $1,000;
one for $2,500 to Trinity Church, June 8, 1767, New-
port; one to the First Baptist Church, Providence, for
£2,000, in June, 1774, and at different dates to various
other churches.) The plan did not succeed as well as
was expected. After lingering along for years, the grant
was sold to " Peirce & Burgess for $500, and John

Allen was authorized to spend the money in repairing
the house." The "Tin Top," at this period, occasionally resounded with the voices of other ministers beside
that of the pastor, and there are those now living who
remember hearing Dr. Stephen Gano, the pastor of the
First Church, Providence ; President Asa Messer, of
Brown University ; Dr. Benedict, of Pawtucket ; Rev. J.
Pitman, and others, within its walls.   On the 10th of September, 1810, the church joined the Warren Association.
The church held their stated Sabbath worship in the
meeting-house until about 1830.   Up to this time various
places were used for evening worship, and frequently,
upon the Sabbath, in Crompton.   Among the buildings
used for such purposes was the old "Cotton House," a
building since removed, which stood just back of the
Crompton Company's stable, and the old "Weave Shop,"
not far from Deacon Spencer's store, on the opposite side
of the road.   Elder Curtis wrote me before he died that
he taught an evening school there, as well as held meetings, and that many of his pupils were there converted.
The "Hall" house, that has since been removed farther
south on the turnpike, opposite the site of the old Cotton
House, was also used for religious purposes, and other
buildings as they could be obtained, up to the time when
the "Store Chamber" was fitted up for a place of
worship.   It is said that the place where the church was
worshipping, at the time Elder Ross was the pastor,
"became too straight for the people, and especially so
for the minister," and larger and better quarters were
provided in the Store Chamber.   This item fixes the
time at about 1830, when they entered the latter place.
The church, from this time, held its regular Sabbath
services in Crompton, instead of Quidnick.   The "Tin
Top" was leased for a time to other worshippers, and
was finally sold at public auction to Wm. B. Spencer,
Esq., in trust for the Rhode Island Baptist State Convention, for the sum of $320.   It still remains in posses-
sion of the Convention, though occupied by the Quidnick
Baptist Church, which was organized in 1851.

*4

Rev. David Curtis, son of William Curtis, was born in East Stoughton, Mass., Feb. 17, 1782. He was educated at Brown University, where he graduated in 1808. He was married to Rhoda Keach, of Smithfield. R. I., June, 1810, by Rev. Dr. Gano. His wife was born June 15, 1790, and died Nov. 26, 1864, at East Stoughton. Elder Curtis died at the same place Sept. 12, 1869. There are two sisters of Elder Curtis now living. He had thirteen children, two of whom are now living. One of his sisters married Rev. George Winchester, a Methodist clergyman. On February 6, 1819, Elder Curtis took a letter from the church and united with that of Pawtuxet. He was pastor at the latter place at two different times, and in 1821–22 was the postmaster. The post office occupied a part of the house in which he lived, which is now standing, and is the first one south of the bridge on the west side of the street. He preached about two years at Harwich, Mass., and about the same length of time at New Bedford. He then removed to Abington, Mass., where he remained about eight years, a part of which time he was the pastor of the church there. He then removed to Fiskeville, R. I., and preached about two years, also about two years at Chepachet. For the last twenty-five years of his life he lived in East Stoughton, preaching as he had opportunity to various churches, but without being settled as a pastor. On the death of his father he was left with some property, from which he derived a comfortable support during the latter years of his life. For many years previous to his death he made an annual pilgrimage to the scenes of his early labors, where he was always welcomed to the pulpit of the church and to the homes of the people.

Elder Curtis was followed in the pastoral office by Rev. Levi Walker, M. D., who united with the church January 2, 1819, though it appears he had preached to the church already two years. Business in the village of Crompton was in a depressed state, growing out of the failure of the manufacturing company, and the church found itself less able than usual to support a pastor. I find on the records of the church a vote by which they agreed to raise for Dr. Walker the sum of fifty dollars for the year. The doctor found it necessary to eke out his small salary by exercising his skill in the healing art. Though the scriptures declare that man shall not live by bread alone, they do not ignore the fact that some bread is necessary. Mr. Walker remained the pastor until December, 1819, and then took a letter and united with the church at Preston, Conn., where he became the pastor.

Dr. Walker was born in 1784. His childhood was spent in Livermore, Maine. He experienced religion about the year 1804, and was for about twelve years a zealous Methodist preacher. His views on the subject of baptism underwent a change, and he united with the Baptist Church in Fall River, then under the pastoral care of Elder Borden. In 1807 he married Phebe Burroughs, a daughter of Elder Peleg Burroughs, pastor of the Free Will Baptist Church, in Tiverton, R. I. Dr. Walker preached in Fall River, New Bedford and Edgartown previous to his settlement over this church. After leaving Preston, Conn., he removed to North Stonington, where he continued to preach and practice medicine until about the time of his death. He died in Winstead, Conn, at the age of 87. "As a preacher he was clear, logical and convincing, rising at times to points of highest excellence, both in matter and manner." He possessed considerable skill as a physician. He had three sons who entered the ministry, viz.: Rev. W. C. Walker, now State Missionary in Connecticut; Rev. Levi Walker, Jr., deceased, and Rev. O. T. Walker, for several years pastor of Bowdoin Square Church, Boston, now pastor of the Third Baptist Church, Providence.

The third pastor, Rev. Jonathan Wilson, received a call from the church to the pastorate April 5, 1823, which he accepted, and united with the church June 8th following, and remained until February 19, 1830. During this period a slight difficulty arose, occasioned by a portion of the church desiring to have a young brother whom the church had licensed, preach half the time and Mr. Wilson the other half. Mr. Wilson went off to the southern part of the State and preached about six months, the Rev. Seth Ewer, an agent of the State Convention, preaching in the meantime. He then returned and resumed his labors to the above date. Elder Wilson is spoken of as an able preacher, but was not thoroughly established in his religious sentiments. He went west and became a Millerite. As late as 1847 he returned to the east, and preached a few weeks in Providence, with the expectation of being soon translated to heaven. It is said he carried his ascension robes with him in his preaching journeys. About this time he made a visit to

Centreville, calling on John Allen, who, doubtless, scratched his elbow, but refused to be converted to the views of his former pastor. His subsequent history is unknown.

The fourth pastor was Rev. Arthur A. Ross, who united with the church July 4, 1830, and closed his labors December 18, 1834. The parsonage house was built by Henry Hamilton for John Allen, in 1831, who afterwards gave it to the church.

Elder Ross was born in Connecticut, October, 1790. Mr. Ross' first settlement was in Thompson, Conn., in 1819, where he remained four years. He was pastor successively at Chepatchet, one or two years; Fall River, Mass., three years; Bristol, Warwick and Coventry Church, First Church, Newport, seven years; Lonsdale, two years; Natick, and the Second, or High Street Church, at Pawtucket, the latter place about two years. He died in Pawtucket, June 16, 1864, in his seventy-fourth year, and was buried in the cemetery of his wife's relatives near Cumberland Hill. During his ministry he baptised over 1400 persons. He was a laborious and successful pastor, a plain, outspoken preacher. While pastor at Newport he published a discourse, " Embracing the Civil and Religious History of Rhode Island," from the first settlement of the island to the close of the second century.

The fifth pastor, Rev. Thomas Dowling, united with the church June 5, 1836 ; closed his labors August, 1840.

Mr. Dowling was born in Brighton, Sussex county, England, April 2, 1809. He is a brother of Rev. John Dowling, D. D., of New York. Baptised by Rev. Charles Carpenter, pastor of the Baptist Church, Somer's Town, London; was licensed to preach in October, 1830, and labored as a local preacher in London and vicinity until September, 1833, when he sailed for this country. Was ordained as pastor of the Baptist Church in Catskill, N. Y., January 14, 1834; become pastor at Trumansburg, N. Y., January 1, 1835, from which place he came to this church. From here he went to the Third Church in North Stonington, Conn., and has continued to labor in that State ever since, (with the exception of two years at Agawam, Mass.,) having been settled as pastor at Willimantic, Central, Thompson, Tolland, and other places. In 1873 he resumed the pastorate at Tolland, where he now resides.

Mr. Dowling probably closed his labors as pastor a short time previous to his taking a letter from the

church, as during the interval preceding the settlement
of the next pastor, Rev. Dr. D. W. Phillips, now President of the Nashville Institute, in Tennessee, but then a
student of Brown University, supplied the church for
about six months, preaching at the Tin Top and the
Store Chamber. Dr. Phillips recently revisited the
scene of his early labors, and preached for the church on
the second Sabbath of June of the present year, receiving
a contribution from the church and Sabbath school of
$72 00 for the work in which he is engaged.

The sixth pastor was Rev. Thomas Wilkes, who united
with the church November 8, 1840; closed his labors
August, 1842.

Mr. Wilkes subsequently removed to the city of New York,
where he ministered to a congregation of Swedenborgians. His
ministry there appears to have been of short duration. The
three principal members of his congregation, from whom he
received his principal pecuniary support, it is said, failed him;
one died, another failed in business, and the third removed
from the city. Of his subsequent history I have no knowledge.

January 16, 1842, six persons were dismissed to unite
with others at Phenix to form a new Baptist church,
and the pastors and three delegates were appointed to
attend the council to be held there on the 20th of that
month.

As we look over the records to learn what measure of
prosperity attended the efforts of the church during this
second period of its history, we conclude that God blest
their efforts abundantly. There were special seasons of
refreshing, to which we shall refer hereafter, and seasons
of spiritual drought; times when they were led to
rejoice, and others when they were in heaviness. Up to
this time the church had a large field to cultivate com-
pared with its present limited one. Previous to 1840
there was no other church of the same order in any of
the villages about us. Since then the churches at
Phenix, Natick, Coventry Central, the present Quidnick
Church, and the one at Old Warwick, have all been
organized. The population was, also, almost entirely
native, where now it is so largely foreign.

The third and last period of its history, extending from 1843 to the present time, is more generally known, and will be considered briefly.

On February 21, 1843, a special church meeting was held in Centreville, but at what house the record does not indicate. At this meeting among those present, now living among us, and as interested in the present progress of the church now as at that time, were Bro. Albert H. Arnold and Deacon Alfred Dawley. " Bro. John Allen made a proposition to the church that he would build a meeting house for them on condition that the church would build a vestry to place the house upon." The church voted to accept the offer. An agreement was then made as follows, Bro. Allen agreed to build a house of wood, " 40 by 50 feet, paint and furnish the same in modern style excepting cushions and lamps." The church agreed to purchase a lot and build a vestry in a style to correspond with the house, furnish it with cushions, lamps, bell, furnace, and also to fence the lot. The agreement was faithfully carried out, and the house in due time solemnly dedicated to God. The lot cost $400 ; $1400 further were expended by the church ; Bro. Allen expended $2300, making the total cost $4100.

The dedication was a season of great joy to the church. Rev. John Dowling, then pastor of the Pine Street Church, Providence, preached the sermon ; Rev. Edward K. Fuller, pastor, Rev. J. Brayton and others participated in the services. Thirty-five years had now elapsed since their first sanctuary, the Tin Top, was dedicated, and now a second temple had been raised and set apart to the same service. As the church reviewed her history she had abundant reason to thank God and take courage.

John Allen, to whom the church was indebted so much from the time of its organization, was one of the constituent members of the church, and for " nearly thirty years" its clerk. Reference has been made to him in connection with the account of the village of Centreville. He died July 26, 1845. His painted portrait is in possession of Mrs. Alexander Allen, of Centreville. He gave the church also the parsonage house and lot, and bequeathed on the death of his widow, the lot of land on the north of it. The following is an extract from his last will devising this land :

"I give and devise to the First Baptist Society in Warwick, the lot of land north of the Parsonage after my wife's decease, the same to be held and possessed by said society, their successors forever, for the use of the pastor of the Warwick and Coventry Baptist Church, in addition to his salary, reserving a passage way to my burial lot."

Mr. Allen in his will devised the lot of land now called Point Pleasant Cemetery, opposite the Baptist Parsonage, and his farm of about eighty acres in West Greenwich, to the American Tract Society; six shares in the Warwick Manufacturing Co., and thirty-five shares in the Providence and Paweatuck Turnpike Co., with several acres of land south of the Baptist parsonage, to the Missionary Union; ten shares in the City Bank, Providence, for the support of a missionary in China; two shares in the Warwick Manufacturing Co., fifty-three shares in the Centreville Bank, and sixteen shares in the Bank of Kent, Coventry, for Home Missions; to the R. I. Baptist State Convention, thirty-four shares in the Bank of Kent, Coventry, and thirty-seven pews in the " Tin Top " meeting house, and twenty-five shares in the Centreville Bank, to the American and Foreign Bible Society—all these bequests to be paid after the death of his wife.

The seventh pastor was Rev. Edward K. Fuller, who united with the church August, 1843 ; closed his labors April 15, 1846.

Mr. Fuller was licensed to preach by the Second Baptist Church, Providence, June, 1836. Ordained by the " Independent" Baptist Church, Pawtucket, (now High street) April 4, 1838, where he remained three years. Was two years General Agent of the R. I. Sunday School Union. After leaving here he was pastor at Somerset, Medford, Reading, in Massachusetts, South Providence, New York City, New London and Jamaica, L. I. Now laboring as an Evangelist. Residence, Providence, R. I.

The eighth pastor was Rev. George A. Willard, who united with the church May 1, 1847; closed his labors July 1st, 1850. Mr. Willard was born in Lancaster, Mass., in 1810; ordained August 29, 1843, at Cummington, Mass., where he preached until 1847. He was pastor at Old Warwick from 1850 to 1859; He opened there a Family Boarding School for Boys, which he kept until 1867, preaching as he had opportunity at Natick and other places; was for some time Town Superintendent of Public Schools. He is at present a pastor at Ashfield, Mass.

The ninth pastor was Rev. Jonathan Brayton, who

commenced preaching to the church Aug. 25, 1850; closed his labors January 1st, 1854.

The tenth pastor was Rev. L. W. Wheeler, who preached about a year. Mr. Wheeler has recently settled as pastor of the Baptist Church in Jefferson, N. H., having removed from Lyme Centre, of the same state. A letter forwarded to him failed of a response. The church after Mr. Wheeler left was destitute of a pastor for a year or more, when Mr. Brayton was recalled and commenced laboring April 1, 1857, and continued until ill health compelled him to relinquish his charge in January, 1859. He however continued to preach occasionally being assisted during the remainder of the year by Mr. C. C. Burrows, a student of Brown University.

Rev. Jonathan Brayton was born at Cranston, June 12, 1811. Baptized at Knightsville, when about sixteen years old, by Elder Pardon Tillinghast. At eighteen years of age he went to Providence to learn the carpenter's trade, where with a few others, he united in the organization of a Six Principle Baptist church, now known as the Roger Williams Church. Assisted in building a meeting-house for the church (which was subsequently burnt.) While at work on the inside of the steeple, he accidentally fell a distance of sixty feet, striking on the staging on the way down, breaking his leg and otherwise injuring him, and was taken up insensible. This concluded his carpentering work and changed entirely his course of life. His thoughts were now turned to study and a preparation for the ministry. Taught school three years in Fall River, preaching during a part of the time at Tiverton, and then went to Hamilton University and took the Theological Course, preaching to the neighboring churches during the time. Here he was ordained by the Faculty. Came east and began preaching in Phenix, in 1841-2, his labors resulting in the formation of the Baptist church in that village. During the winter and spring 119 were baptized; for about two years of his stay at Phenix he preached monthly at Natick, and often at Fiskeville. For several years on account of illness did not preach. In 1851, preached at Quidnick and assisted in organizing a church, preaching half the day at Crompton for upwards of three years. At the conclusion of his labors at Quidnick. went to High Street Church, Pawtucket, and labored a year and a half, when he returned to Crompton Church.

In 1858-9 the meeting house was thoroughly repaired, the galleries cut down, new pulpit put in, &c.

The present pastor, Oliver Payson Fuller, was called by the church December, 1859; commenced labor January, 1860; united with the church March 4th, by letter from the church in Canton, Massachusetts, by which he was licensed; ordained March 7, and continues to preach, *qualis ab incepto.*

Mrs. Audrey S. Briggs, widow of the late James Briggs, died July 27, 1873. In her will, she bequeathed the sum of $50 to the church. Both she and her husband united with the church January 7, 1857, and were devoted members until their death.

In 1866, further changes and improvements were made in the meeting house; the ante-rooms were partitioned off, the orchestra window put in, and a new Mason & Hamlin organ, costing $425 was given by Gen. James Waterhouse. In 1873, the house was again repaired, the interior handsomely frescoed, &c., the whole costing about $1,200.

Christopher C. Burrows, a member of the church was ordained to the work of the ministry July 13, 1863, while a member of Brown University, but did not enter upon a pastorate until 1869, when he settled at Davisville, in this State.

Mr. Burrows was born at Busty, Chautauque County, N. Y., April 23, 1825. While at Davisville, he baptized 112 persons. He resigned his charge at Davisville, in 1873, to take charge of the Broadway, Baptist Church, Providence. He is settled at the present time in Lynn, Mass.

The following persons have been licensed by the church: Samuel Greene, November 20, 1818; Charles Weaver, March 24, 1828; Henry Clark, Feb. 25, 1832; Thomas Tew, April 11, 1837; William Lawless, December 29, 1845.

Samuel Greene never settled as a pastor. He died a few years ago at an advanced age, in Coventry.

Charles Weaver was born in Coventry, April 11, 1803; baptized in Washington Village, February, 1823. Married Diana Northup, June, 1823; commenced preaching at Anthony Village, February 10, 1828: organized a Sabbath School at the "Tin Top" June 1st, 1828; ordained at Fiskeville, April 16,

5

1829; left Fiskeville, in 1833, and was pastor successively at
Plainfield, three years, Voluntown, six years, Suffield, four
years, Norwich, four years, Noank, eleven years and Voluntown, the second time, from 1871 to the present time. In an
interesting letter dated April 13, 1875, Mr. Weaver says he has
baptized 1000 converts, and has "been preaching forty-seven
years, and have never seen a single Sabbath that I was not able
to preach."

Henry Clark was born in Canterbury, Ct., November 12,
1810. He commenced teaching in Centreville in 1829, boarding
in the family of John Allen. In the summer of 1830 he was
baptized by Elder Ross, and united with this church. His first
attempt to preach was in the "Store Chamber" on the day
that he was licensed to preach. In 1834, he married Mary
Dorrance of Anthony Village, who is still living. though their
children. seven in number, have all died. He studied at the
Hamilton Literary and Theological Institution. He was ordained pastor of the church at Seekonk, Mass., in June, 1834,
and remained three years; was pastor successively in Taunton,
for two and a half years from 1837; Canton, Mass., in 1840 to
1842; Randolph, 1842 to 1846, when his health failing, he relin-
quished the pastorate until 1870, when he became pastor at
Kenosha, Wisconsin. In 1872, he settled over the church at
Pewaukee, same State. remaining two years, when he returned
to his former charge in the city of Kenosha, where he still
remains. During his .ministry he has baptized about 300
persons.

Thomas Tew, licensed as above, preached for a while
in different places, and became the agent of the Rhode
Island Temperance Organization. A letter of inquiry
respecting him, addressed to his son, failed of a reply.

William Lawless, though a member of the church
never lived here. His residence being in Bristol, where
he died a few years ago. He was never ordained but
continued to exercise his gifts in public as he had opportunity.

The following persons have served the church as dea-
cons: Alexander Shaw, Palmer Tanner, Caleb Ladd,
Ephraim Martin, Warren Rice, James Tilley, Edwin
Miller, Thomas Tilley, N. T. Allen, Jesse Brown, Ira
Stillman. Pardon Spencer, Alfred Dawley, Asa Cran-
dall. The last three are the present worthy deacons.

N. T. Allen was dismissed by letter to unite with the Phenix
church soon after its organization, and from which he received

a license to preach. He was ordained at Waterford, Conn.
August 1846; was pastor successively, at Groton, six years,
Natick, two years, Jewett City, twelve years. He then returned
to Groton where he has been settled the past six years.

The following persons have served the church as
clerks; Barnabas Greene, John Allen, Whipple A. Arnold, William Brown, Robert Bennett, Pardon Spencer,
and Charles T. Carpenter.

The records fail to give the names of those who have
served as treasurers. Among those of the past twenty
years, are Dea. Pardon Spencer, John J. Wood, Deacon
Alfred Dawley, Peleg Brown, Amos Johnson, James E.
Whitford, and Gideon B. Whitford.

Nearly seventy years have elapsed since the organization of the church. The fathers and mothers have all
departed, but the great truths of the gospel which taught
them how to live and how to die, remain the same for
the instruction of their successors. The word of the
Lord endures forever. In looking over the records I,
find that there has been at least twenty years in the history of this church when at least fifteen persons per year
have been added to its number; six years in which not
less than forty per year were added; three years when
not less than eighty per year were added, and one year
when ninety-three were added. The whole number
added during the whole time has been about eight hundred and forty-five, one hundred and one of whom have
united during the present pastorate, upwards of seventy
of them being by baptism. The present number is one
hundred and ten.

The following is a brief account of the Sabbath School
connected with the Warwick and Coventry Baptist
Church :

The earliest item that I have been able to find of an authentic
character respecting the Sabbath School connected with this
church, is that furnished by Miss Abby Sweet, a lady now in
her 77th year, who says she attended a Sabbath School in the
old weave shop, when she was about thirteen years of age, or
in the year 1811. The school she says was conducted by James
Smith, a man from Connecticut. In the winter of 1816-17,
Major Jonathan Tiffany, who was then the agent or manager

of the mills in Crompton, then called the Stone Factory, represented to Mr. Obadiah Brown, of Providence, the religious needs of the place. Mr. Brown gave a dozen bibles, and two dozen testaments for the use of a Sabbath School which was then in progress. Deacon Shaw was superintendent of the school. It was held in the old weave shop and subsequently in the "Hall" house. For several years after Deacon Shaw left, there was no school, and only at irregular intervals until the summer of 1827, when James Greene became the superintendent, and continued the school through the summer and perhaps, the following summer. It does not appear that the school continued through the winter seasons until it found quarters in the "Store Chamber," in the year 1830, when there were facilities for warming the room comfortably. On the evening of May 25th, 1830, a meeting was held, which adopted the following preamble and constitution:

"WHEREAS, we the subscribers being desirous of improving the morals of the children and youth in our village, and of affording them the means of such instruction as is consistent with the sacredness of the Christian Sabbath; and believing that Sabbath Schools are eminently calculated to effect these objects, we unite in a society and agree to adopt the following

CONSTITUTION.

ARTICLE 1. This society shall be called the Crompton Mills Female Sabbath School Society in Warwick, auxiliary to the Rhode Island Sunday School Union.

ART. 2. Any person may become a member of this society by signing the constitution and paying 12½ cents per quarter.

ART. 3. There shall be a President, Secretary and Treasurer and board of Directors."

The remaining articles prescribe the duties of the officers, and the appointment of a Superintendent and teachers, who were to have the immediate oversight of the school.

The quarterly payments were exacted of those who became members of the society. The Sabbath School was free to all. In some places, in the early history of the Sabbath School work, the teachers were paid as in the week day schools, but it does not appear that any were thus paid in connection with this school.

To this constitution were appended the names of seventy-five persons, of whom Crawford Titus, John J. Wood, James Tilley, Silas Clapp, John Spencer, Jr., George A. Bailey, Pardon Spencer, Jonathan L. Pierce, Jeremiah Randall and Jonathan Steadman, were the first ten. On the evening of May 26, Crawford Titus, acting as moderator, Pardon Spencer was chosen president, for the ensuing year; John J. Wood, treasurer; Leonard Loveland, superintendent; Washington Wilkinson and James Tilley, a Board of Directors. On June 5th, 1830, a series of rules for the government of the school were adopted.*

At a special meeting held August 16, 1830, Crawford Titus, John Spencer, Jonathan Smith, Philip Brayton, Mrs. Titus, Mrs. Remington, Mrs. Whitman, Mrs. Cook, Mrs. Clapp, Mrs. Smith, Miss Lydia Smith, Mrs. Higgins, Mrs. Wood, Mrs. Pearce, were appointed a committee to examine the school. Crawford Titus was appointed Librarian. Elder Ross was requested, by vote, to deliver an address to the school the fol-

---

* As these rules are somewhat unique in character we give them in full.

"Rule 1. The duty of the Superintendent shall be to see that each scholar is in the right class; also to see that there is a teacher to each class; to take the name of each scholar and enter it on his book; also to record the names of the best scholars which the teachers may report to him; and also to see that a chapter is read from the scriptures at the opening of the school, and that it is closed with prayer.

2. It shall be the duty of the teachers of the Testament classes to hear the recitations, and attend to reading in the Testament twice; in spelling twice, and spell out of the book once. The remaining time until the close of the school shall be improved in reading, spelling, conversation, or any instruction the teacher shall find necessary for the improvement of the scholars.

3. Classes reading in the Spelling Book shall read and spell the same number of times as the Testament classes; remaining time to be improved in the same manner.

4. Any scholar behaving in an unbecoming manner, the teacher shall report him to the Superintendent and he shall put him in the bad scholars' class.

5. If by disobedience they continue in the bad scholars' class four Sabbaths, the Superintendent shall report them to their parents.

6. If such scholar or scholars attend the school the next Sabbath after being reported to their parents and behave themselves properly for the day, they shall be received into their former class; if not, at the close of the school, such scholar or scholars shall be dismissed from the school until they will become obedient to its rules.

7. The teachers of those classes which have the privilege of taking books from the library, shall report to the Superintendent those scholars who merit books.

8. Those scholars that attend the school more than nine Sabbaths in a quarter shall be rewarded according to the number of Sabbaths they attend.

9. It shall be the duty of each teacher every Sabbath to endeavor to impress upon the minds of the scholars the importance of obedience to their parents and teachers, of constant and early attendance at school, and good behavior in and out of school, of getting their lessons well and keeping the Sabbath day holy; of not indulging in profane language and lying, nor in any of the vices which youth are exposed to; using such arguments to enforce their instructions as are suited to the capacity of their scholars.

10. It shall be the duty of the Superintendent to read, or cause to be read, these rules at the opening of the school every second Sabbath."

*5

lowing Sabbath. April 9, 1831, Pardon Spencer was re-elected President, Leonard Loveland and Sanford Durfee superintendents; Crawford Titus librarian. At this meeting the admission fee was reduced to twenty-five cents per year, and at the annual meeting the following year the teachers were admitted free. Mr. Durfee continued in the office of superintendent until the year 1848, and was followed by Mr. Jesse Brown for a year or two, when Dea. Pardon Spencer was elected, and continued in office until the spring of 1871, since which time Rev. J. Brayton has filled the office. The other officers at present are Charles M. Scekell, assistant superintendent; Charles T. Carpenter, secretary; Job Spencer, treasurer, and John Northup, librarian.

NATICK FIRST BAPTIST CHURCH.

The church was organized on the 23d of November, 1839, and was composed of sixteen persons of regular Baptist Churches, residing in the village and its vicinity. Alanson Wood was appointed deacon, and Fayette Barrows, clerk. On the 25th of December, following, a council, composed of delegates from the First, Second, Third and Fourth Churches of Providence, the Pawtucket, the Warwick and Coventry, the Arkwright and Fiskeville, and the Quidnesett, assembled and after the usual examination, publicly recognized the body as the Natick First Baptist Church.

The first members received by the new church were Pardon Spencer and his wife, Sybil Spencer who were received Jan. 26, 1840, by letter from the Exeter Baptist Church, the hand of fellowship being given by Rev. S. S. Mallory. The first member received by baptism was sister S. Thornton, who was baptized by Rev. Thomas Tew, May 24, 1840. The church was received into the Warren Association, Sept. 9, 1840. On Nov. 16, of this year, Rev. Arthur A. Ross accepted the invitation of the church to become its pastor, "while he continues in this village." This pastorate of Mr. Ross appears to have been of short duration, as on Feb. 18, 1841, the church appointed "a committee to supply the pulpit." At the same meeting, George K. Clark was appointed a deacon. On June 25, 1841, Smith W. Pearce was elected clerk, and served in that capacity until he was appointed deacon, Dec. 25, 1847. April 14, 1842, Samuel Peterman was appointed deacon in place of Deacon Wood, who had removed from the village. The year, 1842, was a prosperous year to the church, during which time a large number united with the church, among them some who continued many years to be the faithful burden bearers of the church. On March 20, 1843, the church invited Rev. Jonathan Brayton to the pastorate of the church; Mr. Brayton accepted and continued in this relation until June 23, 1844. He was also pastor at the same time of the Phenix Church.

On April 25, 1847, Rev. Arthur A. Ross was again called to the pastorate of the church. In June, 1849, Moses Whitman was appointed the Trustee of the Relief Fund. This fund was raised by voluntary contributions, for the relief of the poor connected with the church. On December 4th, 1851, Rev. Stephen Thomas, who had previously been connected with the Six Principle Baptists, and had changed his views to those held by this church, was invited to assume the pastoral care of the church. Mr. Thomas accepted the invitation and was publicly installed as pastor, June 2d, 1852. He continued to preach until Rev. N. T. Allen commenced his labors. Mr. Allen became pastor January, 1855, having preached for the church several months previous to that date. He resigned Nov. 4, 1855.

Rev. A. Sherwin was publicly recognized as pastor of the church, July 2, 1856, and remained one year, when he resigned and became pastor of the High Street Baptist Church at Pawtucket. For about six months following the resignation of Mr. Sherwin, Rev. O. P. Fuller, then a student of Brown University, supplied the church, and until the Rev. Geo. Mathews commenced his labors. The closing part of the year 1857, was the year of the general revival throughout the country, and this church shared in the spiritual blessings, forty-one

persons uniting with the church by baptism. Mr.
Mathews accepted the pastoral care of the church, March
30, 1858, and resigned April 9, 1859.

From this time until the fall of 1863, the church was
supplied by different persons, chiefly by Rev. Harris
Howard, who finally left to accept a commission as chap-
lain in the army. Rev. George L. Putnam was called
to the pastorate Nov. 7, 1863, commencing his labors as
pastor in the December following, and closed in the
autumn of 1865. On Sept. 22, 1866, Rev. J. H. Tilton
was invited to become pastor, and commenced Nov. 18,
1866, closing June 13, 1869. He was followed by Rev.
Charles L. Frost on July 4, 1869, who continued to
preach until July 4, 1875. His wife, Henrietta
Frost, died March 6, 1873. The present pastor, Rev.
Warren S. Emery, was invited by the church to assume
its pastoral care, August 24, 1875.

The following persons have served the church as dea-
cons, viz. : Alanson Wood, George K. Clark, Christopher
S. Warner, Smith W. Pearce, Henry A. Bowen, George
W. Harrington, Moses Wightman and S. H. Tillinghast.

The following persons have served as clerks, viz. :
Fayette Barrows, Smith W. Pearce, John D. Spink,
John W. Money, Henry A. Bowen, Wm. H. Potter and
Byron D. Remington.

On December 27, 1847, the church licensed Deacon
George K. Clark to preach the gospel. On January 12,
1871, the church met with a severe loss, in the death of
George W. Harrington, who had served the church as a
deacon since his appointment, May 2, 1859. Deacon
Harrington was a warm-hearted, sincere christian man,
and is held in grateful remembrance. Early in the present year the church met with a still severer loss, in the
death of Deacon Moses Wightman, who had been connected with the church since 1842. The following ap-
preciative lines are taken from the " *Watchman and
Reflector*," published a short time after his death :—

" In Warwick, R. I., January 15, 1875, Deacon Moses
Wightman, in the 68th year of his age. Brother Wightman, at

the time of his death, had been a respected and beloved member of the Baptist Church, of Natick, for about thirty years. The *Providence Journal*, referring to him, justly says: 'uniting with the church at Natick in early life, he became one of its leading members, and though naturally of a retiring disposition, identified himself with whatever tended to promote the peace and prosperity of the community. Few men in the quiet walks of life, with the advantages he possessed, can hope to accomplish more of real good to a village, than resulted from his simple unostentatious life. With a heart, full of warm tender emotions, kind and sympathizing to those in distress, the village was made better every time he passed through it. Dea. W. was a peace maker, both within and without the church; wise in counsel, though not forward in giving advice; upright and honest from principle; cheerful without levity; active, humble and consistent, in his religious life.' At his funeral brief addresses were made by his pastor Rev. C. L. Frost, of Natick, Revs. O. P. Fuller and J. Brayton, of Centreville, with prayer by Rev. G. Robbins, of East Greenwich. He leaves a deeply afflicted widow and one daughter, members of the same church. May the household of faith, so long and tenderly united, which has 'reason to mourn and reason also to rejoice,' be eventually reunited where the mourning will be lost in eternal rejoicing.''

SHAWOMET BAPTIST CHURCH *

In the spring of 1842, Rev. Jonathan E. Forbush commenced to labor here under the patronage of the R. I. Baptist State Convention. Some religious interest was awakened, and the statement of facts preliminary to the organization of the present church says there were some conversions and baptism. Into what church these converts were baptized is not stated. Doubtless not the " old" church here, which is represented as indeed old and ready to vanish away. Mr. Forbush's work was to establish something more vigorous and vital than that seemed to be.

The first record of a meeting looking to a church organization is without date, but it was probably in September or October, 1842. Five brethren and eleven

---

* The sketch of this Church is from the pastor, Rev. J. T. Smith.

sisters met at the residence of John W. Greene. This meeting, besides consultation and prayer, appointed a committee of three to wait upon the Old Baptist Church and confer with them in reference to the proposed movement, and adjourned to November 2, at same place.

At the adjourned meeting the committee of conference with the "Old" Baptists reported—what, the record does not show, but it was unanimously resolved to push the church project; November 16, was set for the recognizing council, and the churches to be sent to were specified. A committee was appointed to report at an adjourned meeting, Articles of Faith. At that meeting held Nov. 9, the committee reported the New Hampshire Articles, as then published, which were adopted. Two sisters related their experience, and were received for baptism.

Nov. 16, 1842, the Council assembled, as called, at the Old Warwick Baptist Meeting House. It was constituted as follows:—

First Providence.—Brethren, Pardon Miller, Hugh H. Brown, Oliver Johnson.

Second Providence.—Rev. Edward K. Fuller, brethren John Clemmons, John T. Lawton.

Third Providence.—Rev. Thorndike C. Jameson, brethren N. Mason, William C. Barker.

Pawtuxet.—Rev. —— Bowen, brethren R. N. Niles, Remington Smith.

Lippitt and Phenix.—Rev. J. Brayton, brethren R. W. Atwood, Nicholas T. Allen, Wm. B. Spencer.

East Greenwich.—Rev. J. H. Baker.

The Council, which had for Moderator, Rev. T. C. Jameson, and Rev. E. K. Fuller, Clerk, took the customary action in such cases, and adjourned for public services of recognition, at 2 o'clock same day. It was duly held, Rev. J. H. Baker reading scriptures, Rev. T. C. Jameson preaching, Rev. E. K. Fuller offering prayer of recognition, Rev. J. Brayton giving the Hand of Fellowship, Rev. — Bowen addressing the Church, and Rev. J. E. Forbush offering the concluding prayer.

The Church was constituted with thirteen members, whose names follow :

Rev. J. E. Forbush, (Pastor), Eliza H. Forbush, Benjamin Greene, Frances Greene, John Holden, Hester B. Holden, Welthy Potter, Sarah Potter Greene, Sally Greene, Elizabeth Stafford, Waite Lippitt Greene, Sally Holden Low, Sally Low Holden.

Four of the above list survive, and are still members of the church, viz.: John Holden, Hester B. Holden, Sally Greene, and Sally H. Low.

At the first meeting of the recognized church, Benjamin Greene was chosen Deacon, and John Holden, Clerk.

In March, 1845, Mr. Forbush closed his labors as pastor, removing to Westminster, Mass. During these two and a half years, the church was increased by two baptized and three added by letter. Two were dismissed and one died, leaving two, net gain—15 members. In September, of the same year, the church united with the Warren Association.

Rev. Alfred Colburn was Mr. Forbush's successor for three years from October, 1845. In this period, some revival interest brought eight additions to the church by baptism, and one by experience. Seven were also added by letter. There being only one diminution, dismissed ; the net result was a doubling of the membership, 30.

In April, 1848, John W. Greene was elected clerk, holding and honoring the office until April, 1873, since which time the pastor has served as clerk.

After a year and a half of pastoral vacancy, in April, 1850, Rev. George A. Willard, commenced the longest pastorate of the church's history, nine years, closing in May, 1859. It was not only long (for this church,) but measurably prosperous. Nearly every year of its continuance, there were conversions and baptisms.

In 1851, the parsonage house was built at an expense of $1,400, on a half acre lot, the gift of Warren Lippitt, Esq., of Providence. At the same time the church was incorporated under the name of the "Shawomet Baptist. Church, of Warwick."

The changes in membership in the church in these nine years were : Additions by baptism, 28 ; by letter, 3—31. Diminutions, 14 dismissed, and 7 died—21. Increase, 10, leaving a total of 40.

In April, 1859, Deacon Benjamin Greene, removing from the place and the church, was succeeded in his office by Brother John W. Greene, who held it till March, 1871, when he was succeeded by the present Deacon, Elisha Farnham, who is also Sunday School Superintendent.

For about three years, commencing March, 1860, Rev. Henry G. Stewart served as pastor. In this time, there were added 3 by baptism, 1 by experience, and 4 by letter—8. There were 4 diminutions, 1 death, 2 dismissions, and 1 exclusion ; leaving a membership of 44.

After one year of supplies, Rev. E. Hayden Watrous commenced service as pastor in March, 1864. His brief term of two years—he resigned in February, 1866, to go to Lonsdale—was marked by the most fruitful revival in the history of the church. The baptisms were 18 ; and 5 were added by letter—23. The diminutions in the same time were 13 ; 5 by death and 8 dismissed, leaving a net increase of 10, and a membership of 54.

From March, 1866, Rev. Charles H. Ham, of Providence, served the church one year, as stated supply. In this year, 1 was baptized, 4 dismissed, and 1 died ; leaving a membership of 50.

For a little more than two years, until November, 1868, the church depended upon temporary supplies. During this period, there were no additions, while there were 8 diminutions ; 3 by death, 4 by dismission, and 1 by exclusion, reducing the total to 42.

In November, 1868, the church invited Rev. J. Torrey Smith, of Woodstock, Ct., to assume the pastoral charge. Without accepting the call, he served them as stated supply till July, 1869, when he accepted and removed hither.

The present pastorate, has been a term, largely, of discouraging up hill work, relieved occasionally by fea-

tures of success. No large revival has been enjoyed, yet
the word has not been without as positive and marked
fruit as is ever seen. During the six years there have
been two seasons of increased religious interest, resulting
in 16 additions by baptism. There have been also 6
additions by letter—22. The diminutions in the six
years have been 15—12 dismissed, and 3 deaths. Net
increase, 7 ; which makes the present membership, 49.
(This is two less than our last report, but this is the
present number by the list.)

At the commencement of the present pastorate, exter-
nal conveniences for the support of worship were very
defective. The parsonage had been built twenty-four
years, and had never received much repair. During Mr.
Willard's occupancy of it, a boy's boarding school was
kept in it, and after Mr. Stewart left, it was occupied, not
by a pastor, but by temporary tenants, until 1869.
Thorough repairs being needed, more than five hundred
dollars have been raised, and expended upon it.

For the first thirty years of the church's history it had
no place of worship which it could, in any sense, call its
own. The " Old Warwick Baptist Meeting House "
was built in 1829 by proprietors, by whom, as a corporation, under that name, it is owned and held. The
charter gave a privileged use to the Baptist Church of
the place, which, at that time, was the Six Principle
Church, in its waning condition.

When this church was organized in 1842, the Six
Principle Church being quite feeble, and hastening to
its apparant extinction, a considerable proportion of the
members and families interested in the new organization
were proprietors in the house. Quietly and by general
consent this body succeeded to the use of the house,
which they continued to use without interruption, as if
it was their own. But by 1870 it had got quite out of
repair, and was hardly comfortable or decent to use.
But the proprietors could not be brought to any united
action to repair it. The proprietors in the church were
unwilling to spend their money upon a property which

6

the church had no corporate right or interest in. A project for building a house for the church, on a lot given them for the purpose by Marshall Woods, Esq., of Providence, failed of accomplishing anything for want of a sufficient and united interest in it. Nothing, then, remained but to repair and use the existing house ; and this must be done, or the church must abandon her work.

To remove the obstacle which stood in the way of the previous effort of repairing, it became necessary to give the church, as a corporation, the essential ownership of the house. This was done by obtaining from individual owners of pews (*i. e.*, proprietors,) a transfer of their ownership to the church. By this means the church became a large and the controlling proprietor in the house. This being effected, there was no difficulty in securing a vote to repair the house, and assess the expense as a tax upon the pews. It was done to the expense, including a furnace for heating, of about $1,800. Some additional expense for furnishing was provided through the church. For these repairs of meeting-house and parsonage in these six years the church has expended above $2,000, holding its parsonage property and fully three-fourths of the meeting-house property as its own, free of debt. Four thousand dollars would be a moderate estimate of the value of this church property. Looking at the numbers and the resources of the church, it seems like so much created out of nothing.

A summary of the history shows the whole number of persons connected with this church, during these thirty-two years, to be 119. Of these were—

Constituent members	13
Added by baptism	76
Received by letter from other churches	28
Received on experience	2—119

Of these—

Died while connected with the church	20
Dismissed to other churches	48
Excluded	2
Present members	49—119

This summary shows that this church has been

literally a recruiting station. The great bulk of its membership have been baptized on the field. It has dismissed to other churches nearly double the number it has received from other churches, and within one of the number it retains in its own connection.

PHENIX BAPTIST CHURCH.

In the autumn of 1841, Rev. Jonathan Brayton, then under appointment as a missionary of the R. I. Baptist State Convention, "to labor at Natick and vicinity," conferred with one of the residents of Phenix in reference to holding religious services in that vicinity. At the October meeting of the Convention, held in Wickford, the subject was brought up, and the Board appointed the Rev. Thomas Wilkes, then pastor of the Warwick and Coventry Church, a committee "to look over the ground and see how much money could be raised to support preaching." Mr. Wilkes visited the villages of Phenix and Lippitt, and obtained subscriptions to the amount of $30, and meetings were immediately commenced in the school house.

At the opening of the year 1842, a protracted meeting was commenced in the school-house, which soon became so interesting that all who wished to attend could not be accommodated. They then applied to the Methodist society, who were then occupying the "Tatem" meeting-house, owned by Deacon Josiah Chapin, of Providence, for permission to occupy that house, which was courteously granted for two weeks. "As the presence of God was visibly felt, and some souls were converted almost as soon as the meetings commenced, the brethren and sisters, (twenty five in number,) members of regular Baptist churches residing in the vicinity, on the evening of January 10, agreed to organize themselves into a church of Christ, and were publicly recognized as such, by appropriate religious services, on the 20th of the same month.* The recognition services were held in the Tatem meeting-house before the two weeks granted them had expired. Rev. J. Dowling, D. D., preached the sermon; Rev. John H. Baker offered the prayer of recognition; Rev. Thomas Wilkes gave the hand of fellowship, and Rev. J. R. Stone gave the charge to the church. The church assumed the name of "the Lippitt and Phenix Baptist Church of Warwick, R. I." The male members who entered into the organization were the following: Jonathan Brayton, Thomas S. Wightman, William B. Spencer, Jeremiah Franklin, John B. Tanner, Benjamin Gardiner, Richard Gorton, Stephen Greene and Robert Card; the female members were Weltha Spencer, Susan C. Tanner, Abby L. Tanner, Amey Franklin, Susan Albro, Mary W. Johnson, Mary A. Snell, Penelope Thurston, Mary A. Griffin, Martha Shippee, Susan Greene, Abby A. Gorton, Eda Gorton, Phebe Frye, Mary Card, and Mary Pearce. There were nineteen other accepted candidates for admission, making a total of forty-four. On January 30th, twenty-nine persons were baptized, and the ordinance of baptism was administered for three successive Sabbaths afterwards. From January 30 to March 6, seventy-seven persons were baptized and united with the newly formed church.

Soon after the recognition of the church, the time having expired during which they were allowed the use of the Tatem meeting-house, they returned to the school-house, which was found too small to accommodate those who wished to attend. Arrangements were soon made with a view of building a meeting-house, and a committee appointed to attend to the matter. The lot was generously given by the Manufacturing Company, and the committee contracted with Dea. Charles Shaw, of Providence, to build a house, thirty-six feet by forty-eight feet, for $1800. The church built the foundation walls and painted the house. The house was owned by

---

* Minutes R. I. Baptist State Convention, April, 1842.

stockholders, who were to receive interest on the money contributed. The vestry was not finished for use until several years after the upper room was occupied. After the vestry had been fitted up and other improvements made, it was found that the whole expense had amounted to about $3000. The stock subsequently became the property of the church by gift and purchase, and thus remained until the meeting-house was sold.

Rev. Jonathan Brayton was the first pastor, continuing as such seven or eight years. "Rev. Frederick Charlton served the church about nine months, followed by Rev. George D. Crocker, for about the same length of time." Christopher Rhodes also supplied the church for several months, coming from Providence on Saturday, and returning the following Monday. Bro. Rhodes was then a surveyor of lumber in Providence, and devoted his Sabbaths to supplying destitute churches. The church were so well pleased with Bro. Rhodes, that they obtained his promise that if he should decide to give up his secular business and settle as pastor over any church, he would come to Phenix, a promise that he afterwards fulfilled.

In 1851, Rev. Benjamin F. Hedden, became pastor of the church, and continued thus for nearly four years, and was followed by Rev. Christopher Rhodes, whose pastorate continued from April, 1855, for about six years and a half.

In 1852, several of the brethren united and built a house for the pastor to live in, and rented it to the church, which arrangement continued until June, 1870, when the parsonage became the property of the church.

During the pastorate of Mr. Rhodes, the congregation had so increased that it was deemed advisable to either enlarge their house of worship, or to build a new one, and on March 5, 1859, they "voted, that it is expedient to enlarge our meeting-house," and a committee composed of Wm. B. Spencer, S. E. Card, and S. H. Brayton, were appointed to attend to altering and enlarging the house. After examining the house, it was thought

*6

best to sell it and build a new one. " March 19th, 1859, it was voted, that the building committee appointed on the 5th inst., be authorized and empowered to dispose of the meeting house and lot, or any part of the same, if they deem it for the interest of the church to do so, and on such terms as they think best, and if sold, they are hereby authorized to procure another lot and erect a meeting-house thereon, of such dimensions as will meet the wants of the church and society, the plans of said house being first approved by the church." The committee accordingly sold the meeting-house and lot for $1700, the church occupying it for the last time, October 2, 1859. At a meeting of the church, held August 6, 1859, " voted, that the committee appointed to sell the meeting-house and build a new one, be empowered to build such a house of worship, as in their judgment they think best." The lot upon which the church now stands was given by William B. Spencer. The committee contracted with Post & Tuesdell, of Rockville, Conn., who failed of carrying out the contract, when the matter returned to the committee, and after various delays the house was finally completed. The whole amount expended on the meeting-house and lot was $18,437.41. This included $325 for the clock, ($250 of which was generously given by Henry Howard, Esq.,) and a bell, weighing 1,609 pounds and costing $575.49. The vestry was occupied by the church, January 29, 1860, and the upper portion of the house in September, 1869. " It is a capacious and beautiful structure, with a steeple whose height is 162 feet from the ground. The edifice is not only an ornament to the village, but will compare favorably with any village-meeting house in the State. The church may well congratulate itself on the value of its church property, owning also a commodious parsonage; all of the property being entirely free from debt."

At the January session of the General Assembly, 1860, the name of the church was changed to " The Phenix Baptist Church."

In October, 1861, Rev. Bohan P. Byram, now settled

in Plymouth, Mass., became pastor, and remained until
October, 1867. Rev. T. W. Sheppard, the present
pastor, began his labors in April, 1868.

The following persons have served the church as deacons: Thomas S. Wightman, John B. Tanner, Ray W.
Atwood, J. Bailey, J. S. Kenyon, A. J. Burle on, W. T.
Pearce, and W. W. Remington, the last four being now
in service.

The following have served as church clerks:—Wm.
B. Spencer, Hiram Arnold, Wm. B. Spencer, a second
term, and Vernum A. Bailey, the present clerk.

In 1843, Nicholas T. Allen was licensed to preach,
and in October, 1869, Henry V. Baker was also licensed
to preach.

The present number of members is 220.

THE " ELDER TATEM CHURCH," PHENIX.

The exact date of the organization of this church I
have not been able to learn. In 1827, Elder Henry
Tatem occupied the school-house, and until the erection
of his meeting-house in 1829. This church edifice was
the first one built in the vicinity. The lot on which it
stood, the same one now occupied by the Methodist
church, was bought of Mr. Henry Snell, for $120. An
act of incorporation was granted by the General
Assembly at its January session, 1833, to Henry Tatem,
Nicholas G. Potter, Benjamin R. Allen, Caleb Potter,
Sheldon Colvin, Cyril Babcock, Ray W. Atwood, Cyrus
Manchester, Jr., George P. Prosser, Reuben Wright and
William Warner. Elder Tatem preached in this meeting-
house until difficulties broke out which divided the
church in 1837, when Elder Nicholas Potter succeeded
him for a few months. Elder Tatem was ordained in
1816. The society became so feeble, they were obliged
to sell their meeting-house which was purchased by
Josiah Chapin, Esq., of Providence, in behalf of the
Congregationalists. · Rev. Russell Allen became the

preacher under the new regime. Soon the Methodists hired the house, and in 1842 effected its purchase. It stood on the site of the present edifice erected by that society, until it was purchased by Governor Harris, who removed it to another part of the village, and altered it into tenements where it now stands. A published statement of the church now before me, designates it as the "First General Baptist Church in Warwick." It appears to have held to the denominational tenets of the Free-Will Baptists. A copy of the "Minutes of the first meeting of the Rhode Island Union Conference, held in Cranston, October 13 and 14, 1824," gives the names of the pastors and delegates of these churches as comprising the conference at that time, Elder Henry Tatem, of the Cranston Church, Elder Ray Potter, of the Pawtucket Church, and Elder Zalmon Tobey, of the "Fourth Baptist Church, in Providence." In their circular letter published in their minutes, they say, "We are confident that the real followers of the Lamb of equal piety and usefulness in the church may be found for instance among Calvinists and Arminians, notwithstanding their disagreement in opinion. We dare not, therefore, call that common and unclean which God has cleansed."

FIRST FREE-WILL BAPTIST CHURCH.

This church was originally located in that portion of the town now becoming known as Greenwood, near the "High House," so called. Previous to the building of the meeting-house, meetings were held in a school-house, across the railroad, on or near the site of the present new dwelling of Mr. Collingwood. Elder Reuben Allen appears to have been the first pastor, and John Carder and John Gorton deacons. The church was prosperous under the leadership of Elder Allen, and many were added to the church. The church built their meeting-house about the year 1833. Elder Allen was followed in the pastorate by Elder James Phillips, who preached

for several years. The church during this time passed
through severe trials from which it never fully recovered.
Elder Champlain preached for a while in the meeting-
house and until about the time the church of which he
was pastor built a house for themselves about a mile to
the southward. Elder Joseph Whittemore preached
twice a month for a while, about the year 1842–3, and
after that preaching services were held only occasionally
until the house was removed to Pontiac and the church
re-organized.

About the year 1850, the meeting house was removed
to Pontiac upon land given by David Arnold. The
land according to the terms of the deed, was to revert
to the original owner or his heirs, assigns, &c., when no
longer used for church purposes. In March, 1851, the
church was re-organized under the name of The First
Free-Will Baptist Church of Warwick. The following
persons composed the new organization: Joseph B.
Baker, Edmund L. Budlong, Moses Budlong, Wm.
Tibbitts, Burden Baker, John Vickery, Stephen Luther,
Freelove Wood, Hannah Searles, Susan Bennett and
Susan Baker. Uriah Eddy, who united a few weeks
later was appointed a deacon, and Edmund L. Budlong,
clerk. Elder Reuben Allen, who appears to have been
the first preacher under the old organization, was the first
pastor under the new order of things. On March 13, 1852,
the church voted to change their name to the " Warwick
Church." In 1852, Uriah Eddy became the church
clerk. On April 19, 1856, passed a " vote of thanks"
to Elder Reuben Allen for his services during the past
year, and appointed Joseph B. Baker a committee to
supply the pulpit. From this time up to April, 1859,
the pulpit was supplied by different preachers. At this
latter date, it was voted " that Elder Reuben Allen be
our pastor for the ensuing year." On April 28, 1861,
George T. Hill was licensed to preach the gospel, and
on September 6 following, he was ordained as pastor of
the church, by Elders George T. Day and Reuben Allen.
On October following, Horace Thompson was licensed

to preach the gospel. On April 27, 1862, George
Budlong was appointed a deacon. On July following,
Elder Reuben Allen was again chosen pastor for the
ensuing year. On April 26, 1863, Franklin Potter was
licensed " to improve his gift." On June 4, 1864, the
church voted that " David Culver be the pastor for the
coming year, and that an effort be made to raise $200
for his support."

From March 30, 1866, Abraham Lockwood was the
clerk, and Bro. A. Warner, of Providence, became the
preacher. R. E. Fisher was the clerk in 1869. The
last pastor was Elder James Tobey, who preached about
two years. Elder Tobey continued to preach until April,
1869, when failing health induced him to resign, and
from this time until they disbanded, the church was
pastorless.

On November 5, 1871, the church met in covenant
meeting, and expressed its deep sorrow at the recent
death of Deacon Uriah Eddy.

On November 6, 1871, " a council of ministers were present
to confer with the church in regard to the propriety of uniting
with the Apponaug Church. A quorum not being present, the
meeting was adjourned to meet at the church Sunday next, at
2 o'clock P. M. November 12, 1871, church met according to
appointment, and voted to adopt the following resolutions:

To adopt the recommendations of the council held at the
previous meeting, to wit:—

To unite with the Apponaug Church in a body, so many as
can feel it a duty to do so.

Voted, That a list of the non-resident members be transferred
to the non-resident list of the Apponaug Church, in order that
none by this act be left without church connection.

Voted, That H. C. Budlong be authorized to draw up a paper
for the members of this church to sign as an application of
membership in the Apponaug Church.

Voted, That H. C. Budlong present to the Apponaug Church
the records of this church, with a list of applications to that
church; also, a list of all who have taken letters, and a list of
non-resident members of our church, and recommend and pray
them to take them under their especial watch-care, and influence them, as soon as their whereabouts can be learned, to
unite with some evangelical church."

In accordance with the above recommendations, a

portion of the church united with the Free Baptist
Church at Apponaug, and others with other churches,
and the body ceased to be a distinct church. The meeting-house, which was owned by stockholders, was sold
to the colored church, on the Plains,—they having lost
their house by fire,—for $800, who removed it, in 1873,
to the site of their former house, where it now stands.

WARWICK AND EAST GREENWICH FREE–WILL
BAPTIST CHURCH.

The meeting-house of this church is situated on the
Plains, about half a mile north of the village of Apponaug. From the records of the church and other
sources, we subjoin the following account of its origin
and history :   Previous to the building of their meeting-
house, the church, which was organized December 28,
1841, worshipped in various places, but chiefly in the
meeting-house a mile north, near the " High House."
Rev. Geo. Champlain was the pastor, and continued in
this relation for some fifteen years. About the time of
the " Dorr war," the larger portion of the members were
on the side of the " law and order " party, and the
church worshipping in the meeting-house to the northward were largely of the number known as " Liberty
men."   As a consequence of the disagreement in politics
between the two churches, the privilege of holding
meetings in the meeting-house was denied Mr. Champlain and his church, and measures were taken to build
for themselves a house of worship.   Gov. John Brown
Francis, Judge Dutee Arnold and Geo. T. Spicer, Esq.,
now of Providence, but then of Pontiac, interested themselves in their behalf, and a subscription was started to
raise the necessary funds for the erection of a meeting-
house.

The subscription paper was drawn up by Gov. Francis,
and is still preserved.   The following are extracts from
this paper :

" This house is to be consecrated to the use of the Free-Will

Baptist Church of Warwick and East Greenwich, of which George Champlain is now the elder, and Joseph Babcock, deacon; subject, however, to this condition, viz.:

That the seats shall be free for all the worshippers of that congregation, and that no pews shall be erected therein.

It is understood, likewise, that the lot whereon the building is to be located shall be conveyed to the above society, but not until an act of incorporation is first obtained."

Appended to the paper are the follownig names of those who subscribed $20 or upwards, viz.: Judge Dutee Arnold, in behalf of himself and his daughter Marcy, $50; Hon. William Sprague, in behalf of himself and his daughter, Mrs. Susan Hoyt, $75; Gov. Francis, in behalf of himself and his daughter Anne, $75; John Carter Brown, of Providence, $50; C. & M. Rhodes, $25; George T. Spicer, $20.

The land on which the house was built was given by Stephen Budlong to the church. The house was built in 1844, at a cost of $1,275. This house was used until August, 1872, when it was totally consumed by fire. The present house, which is the same one that originally stood near the " High House," and was subsequently removed to Pontiac, was purchased by this society the same year their house was burnt, for $300, and removed to its present position.

The relation that those who have preached sustained to the church is not very clearly defined in the records, so that it is difficult to tell by them whether those who preached were formally recognized as pastors or only supplies. The church has not always, if ever, been able to support a pastor, and has, consequently, been obliged to secure such preachers as were able to support themselves wholly or in part. Among those who have preached to the church for the longest periods, were Elder George Champlain,* Elder E. Bellows, Elder

---

* Elder Champlain became well known throughout the town as quite an able preacher. He was a man of more than usual natural ability, and a forcible speaker, and many anecdotes are told respecting him that reveal his keenness and ready wit. It is said that one time some of his hearers complained to him that he was too personal and

Peter Noka, Elder Benjamin Roberts, Elder Durfee, Elder John Dixon, and the present pastor, Elder Wm. Devereaux, who has preached to them for several years past.

The following persons have served the church as deacons, viz.: Joseph P. Babcock, Job Frye, James B. Waite, Henry E. Sambo, Geo. Champlain, Jr., Samuel S. Bliss, Jeremiah G. Dailey, Thomas H. Brown, Harrison G. O. Lincoln, and others.

The following persons have served the church as clerks, viz.: James B. Waite, Henry E. Sambo, Thomas H. Knowles, Wm. H. Briggs, Samuel B. Eddy, John F. Champlain, John O. Lincoln, Albert G. Lippitt and John P. Gardner.

CENTRAL FREE-WILL BAPTIST CHURCH OF WARWICK.

This church was organized by Rev. Benjamin Phelon, who, on the third Sabbath in August, 1835, baptized and formed into a church the following individuals, viz.: Alexander Havens, Wm. Harrison, William D. Brayton, Thomas W. Harrison, Elizabeth Wickes, Catherine Westcott and Mary E. Wilbur. Their first deacon was Alex. Havens, and their first clerk, Wm. D. Brayton.

Rev. Benjamin Phelon, now of Providence, was their first pastor, and preached for them at this time about two years and a half. He was followed by Rev. Thomas S. Johnson, who was called to the pastorate of the church in October, 1837, and remained about two years.

severe in his preaching. He replied: "When I am preaching I shoot right straight at the devil, every time, and if any of you get between me and the devil, you will be liable to get hurt." While preaching he would sometimes get quite animated, and his gestures on such occasions would be more forcible than elegant. He occupied the old "Tin Top" at Quidnick for awhile, after it was given up by the church that built it, and, it is said, he would sometimes, while preaching there, jump so high that the audience in front of the pulpit could see his knees. To do this he must have gone up more than three feet into the air. Elder Champlain had some failings, but possessed many excellent qualities.

7

Rev. J. S. Mowry was the next pastor, and commenced his labors November, 1840, closing them in May, 1842. He, in turn, was followed by Rev. Martin J. Steere, who remained three years.

In April, 1849. the church invited Rev. Mr. Phelon to become again their pastor, which invitation he accepted, and he continued to preach until September, 1869.

After this, Rev. J. A. Stetson supplied the pulpit for several months, and until the Rev. E. P. Harris was called to the pastorate. Mr. Harris remained about six months.

The present pastor, Rev. George W. Wallace commenced his labors in September, 1870.*

The number of members at the present time is eighty-seven.

THE NEW JERUSALEM CHURCH.

The following interesting communication, giving the origin of this church, is from Hon. Simon Henry Greene. The personal allusions of the venerable gentleman to his own experience, though perhaps not designed for publication, will not detract from the interest with which it will be perused :

RIVERPOINT, R. I., April, 1875.

REV. O. P. FULLER.

Dear Sir,—Mr. Artemas Stebbins who was well known in Warwick as a Methodist Circuit preacher, about the year 1812, was probably the first to make known the New Church Theology in the town. My home was then in the locality of the town now called Centreville, with my mother, Mrs. Abigail Greene, a devoted, worthy member of the Methodist Church. My father was Job Greene, who died in 1808.

In the autumn of 1811, I was placed at a school from home, returning in 1812. I was employed in business

---

* The sketch of this church is furnished by its pastor, Rev. G. W. Wallace.

in Hartford, Conn. in 1813, returning home again in
1814. In 1815 I engaged in business in Providence,
where I married in 1822, and resided there until 1838,
when my business required a removal of my family to
Warwick, my native town, and a removal was made
accordingly, to where we still reside.

You will thus see how the link which had connected
me with Centreville was severed, and how the most inti-
mate relations with that locality, as to me, were measurably suspended. I had notwithstanding, some knowledge at different times of Mr. Stebbins, his whereabouts
and his occupation. I heard of him, not far from the
year 1815, as travelling and vaccinating for the kine
pock, then having the title of Doctor, and that he had
visited Centreville on such a mission. And if my recol-
lection is right, he was then teaching the doctrines of
the New Church,—and it is not unlikely he may have
preached them publicly at Centreville. Years afterwards I heard of him as settled in Swanzey, Mass.,
where I believe he died. I do not know that he ever
became a minister of the New Church, to preach regu-
larly, or indeed at all, anywhere. He was probably the
first man to make a declaration of the doctrines of the
New Church—called by Swedenborg "The Heavenly
Doctrines of the New Jerusalem," in the town of Warwick.

My own attention was attracted to acquire a knowledge of the doctrines, while living in Providence, at
about thirty-five years of age, but the ideas contained
in them were so new to my mind, that I made slow progress in learning ; my former theological notions block-
ing the way for the entrance of the new truths. I had
been religiously inclined from an early age, and had
read much of theological works, but with all my experience and observation, I could not settle into a rational,
satisfactory belief in any of the systems of theology
which had fallen under my notice, until the writings of
the profoundly learned and eminent scholar and christian,
Emanuel Swedenborg, fell in my way. Apparently by

accident, but really by the ordering of the Divine Providence, I came in contact with a few individuals in Providence who were " receivers of the Heavenly Doctrines," and who held regular meetings for worship and for instruction, at Union Hall, near Westminster street, on which occasions a sermon was read by some one of the members. Occasionally a visit was made us by a minister, who preached and administered the sacraments of baptism and the holy supper. We became members of the Bridgewater, Mass., Society of the New Church, and the pastor, Rev. Samuel Worcester, rendered to us occasional pastoral care and services. His brother likewise, now Dr. Thomas Worcester, then the pastor of a New Church Society in Boston, visited us and preached in Providence. Samuel has been dead several years. Thomas is now living in Waltham, Mass., retired from active life, to much extent, in the ministry, on account of advanced age and impaired health. Both of them were sons of Rev. Noah Worcester, one of the earliest and most noted Unitarian Clergymen in the United States. The sons, however, were compelled wholly to repudiate the peculiar theology of their father

I engaged with Mr. Edward Pike, in the firm name of Greene & Pike, to do business in Warwick, in 1828, which copartnership arrangement continued until his death in 1842. I had conversations with him and his brother David, who is still living, on the subject of the New Church doctrines. They became much interested in them, and procured the " True Christian Religion," the final work on Theology of Swedenborg, and of a great number of volumes previously written and published by him, which they read and became convinced of the truth of those doctrines. I became a member of the Bridgewater Society of the New Church in 1836.

In consequence of the interest the Messrs. Pike and I felt to have preaching in Warwick, Rev. Samuel Worcester was invited to preach in Warwick, and he did so at the " Lippitt & Phenix School House," on the 14th of April, 1837, to an audience of about 175 persons. Many interested listeners to New Church teachings were present. Mr. Edward Pike and his brother David soon afterwards visited Rev. Mr. Worcester's home, and were baptized by him at Bridgewater on the 7th of May, 1837. In due time others were baptized by Mr. Worcester here in Warwick, and a little band were associated together to hold regular meetings on the Sabbath day for worship then held, and now continue to be holden, in a house built by Greene & Pike, to be used for the double purpose of a school-house and a house for public worship.

In 1838, I removed with my family to Warwick, and it was arranged, the pastor co-operating, that I should be appointed and authorized to act as a leader in public worship, in which capacity I have officiated to the present time,—to wit: to the year 1875,—a term of nearly thirty-seven years, being now in the 77th year of my age.

It is obvious to a New Churchman, that the New Jerusalem which John saw " coming down from God out of heaven," is indeed leavening the whole world with the Divine love and the Divine wisdom, raising it by those sublime principles to higher and more exalted spiritual, heavenly states. Those heaven-descended qualities infused into the minds of men enlighten their paths, and say unto them in the benignity of perfect love—" this is the way, walk ye in it." But alas! men generally do not believe that it is the Lord in His second coming, " in the clouds of heaven," who is now standing at the door of their hearts—their affections—and knocking for them to open the door, that He may enter in with His love and wisdom, and establish His glorious kingdom there,—they do not believe that all who have died since the world began have been raised from death unto life, and have been judged, and have become associated in the spiritual world with those in similar states with themselves—whether those states be evil, or whether they be good. " Evil is of hell, and good is of heaven." " The life of man is his *love*." If the love be evil, the life is hellish. If the love be good, the life is heavenly.

Yours truly,   SIMON HENRY GREENE.

*7

FRIENDS' MEETING, OLD WARWICK.*

The first "Monthly Meeting" of the Society of Friends held in Warwick, on record, was at the house of John Briggs, in 1699. Meetings were held subsequently at the house of Jabez Greene, and probably until their meeting-house was built. The Greenwich Monthly Meeting then embraced the towns of Providence, Greenwich, Kingstown and Warwick. The following is from the records of the "Monthly Meeting:"

"At Greenwich Monthly Meeting of Friends, held 4 month, 4th, 1716, it was proposed to build a meeting-house at Warwick, and two Friends were appointed to lay the proposition before the Quarterly Meeting, and also the Yearly Meeting."

Three months later the Monthly Meeting decided to build the meeting-house. The records do not inform us when the house was built, but it appears to have been built before the land upon which it stood was purchased, probably by permission of the owner, and with the understanding that a deed of it would be given. On the "ninth of 3d month, 1720, Benjamin Barton sold to Samuel Aldrich, Thomas Arnold, Jabez Greene, Joseph Edmonds and Thomas Rodman, for £45, current money, one and a half acres and thirty-five rods" of land, "being that piece or parcel of land on which stands a certain meeting-house in which ye people called Quakers usually meet in Warwick aforesaid."

The Friends were never numerous in the town, but held meetings in the house at Warwick frequently during the last century; for the last fifty years only occasionally has the house been occupied. The old meeting-house was so much injured by the September gale of 1815, that it was taken down the following year, and a portion of its timbers were used in the erection of the present

---

* For a portion of the items in the above account, I am indebted to the venerable Perez Peck, of Coventry.

modest structure. The old house was considerably larger than the present one, and was two stories high.

Loyd Greene, an approved minister of the Society of Friends, and a resident in that vicinity, gave the Society the sum of $500, the interest of which was to be expended in keeping the house in repair. This money they deposited in a savings bank, and by the dishonesty of the cashier they lost about one-third of it about ten years ago. The interest has since been allowed to accumulate to the amount of the original sum. Loyd Greene sold his farm at Old Warwick, and removed to East Greenwich, where he became disheartened, and wandered back one day to his old home, and hung himself in the barn which he formerly owned. He is remembered as an upright, conscientious man. The old meeting-house has been thoroughly repaired during the past season, and is one of the oldest buildings in the State occupied by the Friends for their religious meetings.*

EPISCOPAL CHURCH, COWESETT.

The items respecting the church in which Rev. Dr. James McSparran, Dr. Fayerweather, and others, officiated once a month, are gathered chiefly from the interesting work of Mr. Updike.

"On the 2d of September, 1728, a lot of ground situated at equal distances from the present village of Apponaug and East Greenwich, and between the post road and the present Stonington railroad, was conveyed by the Rev. George Pigot to the Society in London for the Propagation of the Gospel in Foreign Parts, for erecting a church according to the establishment of churches by law in New England. A church was accordingly erected,—a wooden building, two stories in height, with a steeple and spire, fronting the post road. After remaining unoccupied a long time, in a ruined state, it was taken down, about the year 1764, by inhabitants from Old Warwick, for the

---

* Their first house at East Greenwich was built in the year 1700, and the first meeting held in it was on the "second of seventh month," of that year. They continued to worship in it until the year 1806, when they erected the one they now occupy.

purpose of erecting a church there. The materials having been conveyed to the shore, were scattered and lost during a storm which arose soon after. A number of graves, probably of individuals connected with the church, are still to be seen upon the lot. The Rev. George Pig t resided in Warwick a number of years, and owned a track of land there. He probably obtained the means of erecting the church."

When the congregation of Trinity Church, Newport, built their new church in 1726, they gave their old building to the people of this denomination living in this town, and, according to tradition, it was floated from Newport to this place. From the abstracts of the Missionary Society, under whose patronage the Episcopal clergymen in this State then acted, we learn that Dr. McSparran officiated monthly in Warwick, from 1741 to 1757, and Mr. John Graves from 1762 to 1783, the former receiving for his services the sum of £50; the latter, £15.

The house stood on the corner of the street that leads down to the "Folly Landing,"* on the site of the house erected a few years ago by Edwin Bowen. The graveyard was just south of Mr. Bowen's house. There were inscriptions on but two of the stones, those of Capt. John Drake and his wife. The Captain, as appears from the inscriptions on the stone erected at his grave, died January 29, 1733. His wife died July 23, 1738. The remains, with the grave stones, were removed to the old Caleb Ladd burial lot, about an eighth of a mile to the northward, many years ago, by Mr. Jonathan N. Peirce, who owned the lot at the time.

This lot subsequently came into possession of David Greene, who sold it to Rufus Spencer, who bequeathed it to his daughter, Mary Spencer. Mary Spencer, by will, gave it to the Society of Friends at East Greenwich. On February 1, 1803, as per deed of that date, Nicholas Congdon, Darius P. Lawton, Perez Peck, Beriah

---

* The origin of this term is as follows: Josiah Baker put up a house near the shore and kept a sort of tavern, which became known as "Baker's Folly." The term "Folly" became applied to the wharf also, and for awhile the railway station near it was so called.

Brown, and others, in behalf of the Society of Friends, sold this lot and land adjoining, amounting to fifty acres, "being the same as conveyed to them by Mary Spencer, late of Greenwich, daughter of Rufus Spencer," to Jonathan N. Peirce for the sum of $2000. A portion of this tract was sold a few years ago to Amasa Sprague for $12,000. A portion on which the old meeting-house stood, Mr. Peirce sold to Mr. Bowen, as above stated. Mr. Peirce, at the ripe age of eighty-three, resides upon a portion of his purchase made in 1808, having removed his house from the opposite side of the road when he sold the land to Amasa Sprague.

The following are extracts from the church records, with biographical comments by Mr. Updike :

"April 11, 1736. Baptized at Cowesett, (Warwick Church), by Mr. McSparrau, two children, viz.: Rebecca Pigot, daughter of Edward Pigot, and Charles Dickenson, son of Capt. John Dickenson."

"Edward Pigot was the brother of the Rev. George Pigot, and was a physician,—came to Warwick soon after his brother, but remained but a few years after his brother removed to Salem."

"Sept. 7th, 1739. Dr. McS. preached at the church in Warwick, and admitted Mr. Levalley to the sacrament of the Lord's supper."

"The Mr. Levalley here mentioned was probably Peter Levalley, who died in Warwick in 1756, and was the ancestor of the Levalleys in Warwick and Coventry."

"Dec. 14, 1745. Dr. McS. preached Moses Lippit's funeral sermon, and buried him in his own ground in Warwick. He died the 12th, about 11 o'clock in the forenoon."

"June 8, 1746. Dr. McSparran baptized by immersion a young woman named Patience Stafford, daughter of Samuel Stafford, of Warwick, and then from Mr. Francis' rode to the church, read prayers and preached there."

"April 21, 1750. Baptized by immersion, in Warwick, Elizabeth Greene, wife of Richard Greene, and by affusion, Welthan Lippit, wife of Jeremiah Lippit, a sister of said Richard."

"Saturday, June 12, 1756. Dr. McSparran administered baptism by total immersion to two young women at Warwick, viz.: Elizabeth Greene, jun. daughter of Richard Greene and Elizabeth, his wife, and to Sarah Hammett, daughter of an Anabaptist teacher, some time ago dead."

" July 23, 1756. As I came home from Providence, I took
Warwick in my way, and baptized by immersion one adult,
named Phebe Low, daughter of Philip Greene, Esq., of Warwick, and wife of one Captain Low."

" Philip Greene was the grandson of Deputy Gov. Greene,
and the father of Col. Christopher Greene, of the revolution,
and married Elizabeth Wickes, sister of Thomas Wickes."

About the only relics connected with the old church
known to exist at present, are a portion of its records,
and a Bible and prayer book, given to the church by the
" Society in London for the Propagation of the Gospel
in Foreign Parts." These latter fell to the possession of
a Mrs. Lippitt, who lately died in Providence. The
books are probably now in possession of the nieces of
Mrs. Lippitt.

ST. PHILIP'S CHURCH, CROMPTON.

At a meeting of several persons, desirous of forming
a Christian congregation in communion with the Protestant Episcopal Church, held in Crompton Mills, Warwick, on the 27th of May, 1845, the Rev. James H.
Eames was appointed chairman, and Mr. David Updike
Hagan secretary. After due deliberation it was decided
to form a religious society to be known " by the name
and style of St. Philip's Church." The following persons were appointed wardens and vestrymen :   Frederick
Pfawner, senior warden ; David Updike Hagan, junior
warden ; Wm. C. Gregory, James Crawford, James H.
Clapp, Thomas Tiffany, vestrymen ; David U. Hagan,
vestry clerk, and James H. Clapp, treasurer.

The vestry were instructed to procure " a lot or lotts
for the use of this congregation as soon as the sum
necessary to effect it shall be subscribed." The present
lot on which the meeting-house is situated was purchased
and the house built during the year. It was consecrated
by Rt. Rev. J. P. K. Henshaw, Bishop of the Diocese
of Rhode Island, January 1, 1846. The house was
never completed according to the design, which contem-
plated a tower and vestibule on one of its corners, with

other ornamentation. The cost of the house in its present form was $1200.

Previous to the building of the church, religious services were held in the " Store Chamber " for about a year, Rev. J. Mulchahey, now assistant rector of Trinity Church, New York, and Rev. Daniel Henshaw, son of the Bishop, and now rector of All Saints Memorial Church, Providence, officiating on alternate Sabbaths. The first baptism recorded on the church records is that of a child of Thomas Hampson, December 19, 1843.

The following is the list of the rectors: Rev. J. Mulchahey; C. E. Bennett, since deceased; G. W. Chevers, deceased; E. W. Maxey, now in New York State; D. Potter, now of Cambridge, Mass.; R. H. Tuttle, now of Connecticut; Silas M. Rogers, now settled in South Lee, Mass.; Robert Paul, in New York State; James S. Ellis, now in Wilkinsonville, Mass., and Thomas H. Cocroft, the present rector.

The Rectory was built by Mr. Cady Dyer for his private residence, and subsequently sold to the Diocesan Convention that holds the church property.

The rectors have been accustomed to hold religious services also in some of the other villages, where missions have been established, as at Fiskeville, Scituate and Phenix. At the latter place, Benjamin C. Harris built a small Gothic building, known as " Little Rock Chapel," which was used awhile for Episcopal services.* In January, 1861, when Rev. Mr. Rogers became the rector, he found a debt of $1300 on the Rectory, which he succeeded in reducing to $440. Mr. Rogers closed his term of service in August, 1867. During the time, he " baptized 111 infants, children and adults ;" 45 persons were confirmed ; 69 persons were buried, and 27 couples married. In 1873, the church was found to be greatly in

---

* This building was afterwards purchased by the Catholics, through the agency of Rev. Mr. Gibson, pastor of St. Mary's, Crompton, for $400. The lot was given by Mr. Harris. It was used for religious services until about the time their present church was obtained, and. then sold.

need of repairs, and in July and August of that year, it was repainted on the inside, the walls were frescoed, and a new carpet purchased, the cost of the repairs amounting to about $400, part of which was contributed at home and the remainder in Providence. After the resignation of Mr. Paul, in 1870, the rectorship remained vacant until Easter of 1873, when the Rev. James S. Ellis, of Delaware, was appointed rector and missionary, who continued in office until July 1, 1874, when the house was closed for some months. Rev. Mr. Cocroft commenced his labors in the spring of the present year.

ALL SAINTS PARISH, PONTIAC.*

This parish was organized April 9, 1869, when the following officers were elected : Senior Warden, Stephen N. Bourne ; Junior Warden, John P. Olney ; Treasurer, John F. Knowles; Clerk, John P. Olney ; Vestrymen, Samuel Black, Samuel Preston, Henry Owen, John Gildard, Edwin R. Knight, William Wooley, Isaiah Wilde, Thomas Evans, Charles S. Robinson, William A. Corey, John F. Knowles.

The services of the Protestant Episcopal Church were held in All Saints Chapel for the first time on Sunday, April 1, the Rev. L. Sears, of St. Bartholomew's Church, Cranston, reading as far as the creed, and the Rev. Robert Paull, of St. Philips Church, Crompton, the remainder of the service, the sermon being preached by the Rev. D. O. Kellogg, of Grace Church, Providence.

The first rector, the Rev. E. H. Porter, commenced his labors in the parish July 4. There were then found to be but five regular communicants of the Protestant Episcopal Church connected with the parish, though at the first administration of the sacrament of the Lord's Supper, there were fifteen participants, most of whom were members of other evangelical churches.

* The account of this church is furnished by John P. Olney, clerk.

After a year of remarkable growth and prosperity, the Rev. Mr. Porter resigned the rectorship of the parish in July, 1870, which resignation took effect October 1.

The Rev. H. K. Browse, formerly of Pennsylvania, was the next rector, remaining in the parish until September 4, 1872, when his ill-health compelled him to give up his pastoral work and send in his resignation.

Rev. Wm. H. Williams took charge of the parish in December, 1872, and remained till April 1, 1875.

The number of regular communicants actually resident in the parish April 1, 1875, is 36. The Sunday School numbers 102. The amount of funds raised for the support of public worship, and other church and Sunday School purposes, during the year ending April 1, 1875, was $1,488 14.

The Messrs. B. B. & R. Knight, of Providence, tendered to the parish in 1869, for church purposes, a room neatly fitted up with sittings and chancel furniture, and also a dwelling for its rector, both free of rental, and also have always been liberal subscribers to the fund for the minister's salary.

METHODIST EPISCOPAL CHURCHES.

There are two flourishing churches of the Methodist denomination in the town, both having their origin in the early part of the present century, but the writer has not been successful in obtaining official accounts of either. One of them, which is probably the older, is located in the village of Centreville, and the other at Phenix. They were supplied for many years, or as late as the year 1825, and perhaps later, by circuit preachers only, and the records of that period are not in possession of these churches. The "Warwick Circuit" included not only these villages, but also those of East Greenwich, Wickford, Plainfield, Conn., and other places, and the preachers were accustomed to pass from one to the other in rotation, on horseback, preaching in school-houses and private dwellings as they had opportunity. In 1830–1,

the church at Centreville built their meeting-house, and
ten years later the church at Phenix were also in possession of a house of worship. But the records of both,
as I am informed, for many years subsequent to these ·
dates, are not now in their possession, nor do they know
what has become of them., Many interesting items connected with their origin and progress would have been
gathered from the older members and presented in this
connection, but for the expectation cherished to the latest
moment, that they would be furnished in connection
with such information as could be obtained from existing
records by some one connected with the churches who is
more thoroughly conversant with their history.

SECOND ADVENT CHURCHES.

There are two churches of this order in the town, the
older one located in the village of Arctic, and the other
at Natick. The church at Arctic held its meetings at
first in Odd Fellows' Hall, in the year 1858. The meetings were conducted by Elder George Champlain, a
colored preacher, who was for about fifteen years the
pastor of the Warwick and East Greenwich Free-Will
Baptist Church on the Plains. He was assisted by Elder
E. Bellows. The meetings at the hall resulted in the
conversion of quite a number of persons, fourteen of
whom were baptized by Elder Champlain on the 26th of
February, 1858, and sixteen on March 14 following. On
the evening of April 6, a church was organized at the
house of Josiah Taylor, consisting of twelve persons.
After the organization, Josiah Taylor and William Smith
were chosen deacons, and John P. Babcock clerk and
treasurer. Elder Champlain was chosen pastor.

It was arranged to have public religious services every
third Sabbath at Odd Fellows' Hall. The business and
covenant meetings were usually held at the house of
Deacon Taylor. On the evening of August 14, 1858,
Elder Champlain's resignation of the pastorate was
accepted, and Elder E. Bellows was chosen his successor.

On October 15, 1858, Alanson Wright was chosen deacon in place of Deacon Smith, who had resigned to go to another part of the country. On November 6, 1858, A. C. Greene was chosen clerk, in place of John P. Babcock, resigned.

At a meeting held February 26, 1860, the subject of building a house of worship was considered. It was ascertained that about $600 had been subscribed for this object, and by vote of the church it was decided to purchase of Mr. Alexander Allen, for the sum of $100, a piece of land 65 feet front by 120 feet deep, as a site for the building; that the house should be 31 feet by 46 feet, 14 feet posts. C. Spencer, Isaac Andrews and Alanson Wright were appointed a building committee, with instructions to erect the house immediately. The land was accordingly purchased of Mr. Allen and the house built. The first meeting—one for business—was held in it on the evening of May 12, 1860. At a meeting held October 19, 1862, Rice Knight, Elisha B. Card and Oliver Crandall were chosen deacons. The last meeting, the proceedings of which were recorded upon the church book, was held December 19, 1863, at which time it was voted to give up the forenoon services and substitute the Sabbath School. Elder Augustus Durfee has been the pastor for some years past, preaching one Sabbath per month. The church has not been able to support a pastor much of the time, and it has been frequently without a regular pastor, depending upon such supplies as they were able to procure.

The church at Natick was organized May 24, 1874, with twenty members. The present number is twenty-three. Spencer H. Shippee and Silas Mitchell were chosen deacons. They hold their meetings in Smith's Hall. Elder Elisha B. Card is the pastor and clerk.

CATHOLIC CHURCHES.

The following communication respecting the churches of this order in Crompton and Phenix is from Rev. Mr.

Gibson, the esteemed pastor of the Catholic Church in the former village:

CROMPTON, Oct. 14, 1875.

REVEREND SIR—

In response to your expressed desire for some information respecting the progress of Catholicity in Crompton, or in my parish, I have collected a few facts and items which I submit to you, hoping they may be of service in the correct compilation of the work you are preparing for publication.

I cannot better commence to narrate the few facts and items I have collected in reference to the history of the Catholic Church in Crompton, than by referring to a work entitled "Sketches of the Establishment of the Church in New England," published in 1872 by Rev. James Fitton, the first pastor of the church in Crompton, and by whom the first church was commenced on September 23, 1844. It relates in condensed form nearly all the important matter concerning its establishment, and I will quote entire the "Sketch" under the heading of the Church of our Lady of Mount Carmel, Crompton:

"Apart from Pawtucket, the largest number of the faithful in any town contiguous to the city, and who were considered as belonging to the charge of SS. Peter and Paul, Providence, were at Crompton. This place having been attended monthly, and the hard-working and industrious operatives in the factory, among whom were those having families of little ones, being anxious to have a place where they might assemble on Sundays, and willing to contribute according to their means, an acre of land was secured September 23, 1844. A small church, a frame building, was immediately erected, and as the location selected was on the hill side of the village, overlooking the country for miles distant, it was styled the 'Church of our Lady of Mount Carmel.'

The congregation of Crompton and its neighborhood was confided to the special care of Rev. James Gibson, who attended occasionally, as his duties at other stations permitted, till August, 1851, when assuming its sole charge he added seven and three-quarters acres to the original purchase, thus making eight acres and three-quarters of land, all enclosed within a substantial stone wall. Besides which, for the better accommodation of the congregation, he has added twenty by fifty-eight to the church, making it one hundred and eight by fifty feet, independent of Sanctuary and Sacristy, twenty by twenty-one, and its tower twelve by twelve, square, and forty-five feet high, with a sweet-toned bell of over 1400 pounds weight. He has also built a pastoral residence of thirty by twenty-eight feet, tastefully and conveniently arranged, and a school-house, eighteen by forty feet, wherein to gather the little ones of his spiritual charge.

He has also lately secured, on what is known as Birch Hill, a very fine building, over thirty-one by forty-five feet, erected originally for a select high school, which he has converted into a neat little church, with its porch of eight by ten and sacristy twelve by fifteen feet."

The above is a very clear and correct statement, and there is little to be added up to the time of the publication of the "Sketches." I would, however, remark that the immediate successor of Rev. James Fitton was Rev. Edward Putnam, and one or two others, who occasionally attended the Crompton church, until the appointment of Rev. D. Kelly, who was the first local, resident priest, and remained in Crompton about nine months, when he was removed and the present pastor assumed the charge.

Since 1844 there has been much progress, and many improvements in the foregoing sketch. The original parish under the charge of one priest only, has increased to such an extent, that it has been divided into five separate parishes, each one with its handsome church and resident priest.

Besides the church of St. James in Birch Hill, in 1870, two acres of land was purchased in Centreville for the erection of a central church at some future time. There is a fine Hall on the grounds, which at present is used for meetings of St. Mary's Brass Band, St. Mary's Temperance Society and other public meetings and social gatherings.

The Cemetery, too, adjoining the Crompton church deserves especial mention. It has been extensively enlarged, improved and adorned in various ways, so that what was originally a crude mass of stones and natural rubbish, has become a lovely retreat, and a beautiful place of christian burial.

There have been other minor improvements, but sufficient has been mentioned to show the wonderful progress of the Catholic church in Crompton since the erection of the "small church" on the hill-side of the village.
Respectfully,

J. P. GIBSON.

PHENIX CATHOLIC PARISH.

This flourishing parish, once a part only of the Crompton church was made into a separate parish in 1858 and
placed in the charge of Rev. Dr. Wallace, now pastor of
St. Michael's church, Providence. He remained there
about seven years. During the first year or two, the
catholic church there was a small building called the Rock
Chapel, being built on a solid rock foundation. It was
formerly an Episcopal chapel, and was purchased by Rev.
J. P. Gibson of Mr. Benjamin C. Harris for the purpose of
converting it into a Catholic chapel. Mr. Harris very
generously gave the foundation and ground around, and
made no charge except a moderate one for the building
alone. But this chapel very soon was inadequate to the
wants of the increasing number of parishioners, and Dr.
Wallace sold it, and purchased of the Baptist society the
church now under the charge of Rev. John Couch, who
resides in Phenix, and has been pastor there since the
removal of Dr. Wallace.   J. P. G.

In addition to the foregoing, for the accommodation of
the large number of French Catholics, a large and handsome church edifice was erected last year near the Centreville railroad station, 112 x 60, which is not yet com-
pletely finished; the large and convenient vestry being
at present used for religious services. It is called St.
John's church, and Rev. Henry Spruyt is the pastor in
charge.

At Natick, too, within the past three years, a church
has been erected to accommodate the catholic residents of
that village, and the resident pastor, Rev. Mr. Reviere,

preaches to two distinct congregations at different parts of the day—to one in English and to the other in the French language.

There has also within the past year, been erected in Apponaug a neat church by Rev. Wm. Halligan, of Greenwich. These comprise the five Catholic parishes of this town.

SUMMARY.

Of the twenty-eight churches that have existed in this town since its settlement in 1642, five have become extinct. Of those still existing, three are of the Six Principle Baptist order ; four are Baptist; two Free Baptist ; one Congregationalist ; one Friends ; one New Jerusalem ; two Methodists ; two Adventists ; two Episcopalian, and five Roman Catholic ; making the present number twenty-three. Besides these, there have been several mission stations established, for longer or shorter periods, and several halls have been used at different times for religious services.

MARRIAGES

BY

ELDER JOHN GORTON,

OF WARWICK.

———◆———

THE list of marriages by Elder John Gorton of Warwick, cover a period from January 1, 1754, to May 4, 1792. The list as here given was printed in a newspaper, the Pawtuxet Valley Gleaner, published at Riverpoint, R. I., during the summer and fall of 1879. In his introduction to the first portion the editor said: "They are 281 in number. The names of the parties married and the dates of their marriages were recorded in this book by Mr. Gorton, who is supposed to have been the only Elder residing in Warwick at that time. He was pastor of the Six Principle Baptist Church, and lived in a gambrel roof house, now standing, and located near the East Greenwich line, on the main road leading from Apponaug to Greenwich." The value of this list as a contribution to the history of the people of the town of Warwick is apparent at a glance.

Anthony Low and Phebe Greene, both of Warwick, married January 1, 1754.

Peleg Rice and Annie Remington, both of Warwick, married May 19, 1754.

Samuel Sweet and Mercy Potter, both of Warwick, married September 23, 1754.

Stephen Greene and Mary Rhodes, both of Warwick, married October 24, 1754.

Caleb Hill, of North Kingstown, and Mercy Stafford, daughter of Stutely Stafford, deceased, of Warwick, married March 23, 1755.

Peter Levalley and Mary Haines, both of Warwick, married May 11, 1755.

John Low and Sarah Wicks, both of Warwick, married October 26, 1755.

John Healy, of Providence, and Ellis Lockwood of Warwick, married July 25, 1756.

James Warner and Rebeckah Low, both of Warwick, married January 6, 1757.

Benjamin Spencer, son of Walter, of East Greenwich, and Sarah Low, of Warwick, married January 20, 1757.

Charles Holden and Hannah Martin, both of Warwick, married January 23, 1757.

Pardon Daly, *alias* Ralph, and Mary Hathaway, both of Warwick, married March 2, 1758.

Joseph Wickes and Bridget Price, both of Warwick, married June 22, 1758.

Peleg Salisbury, of Cranston, and Mercy Sweet, of Warwick, married December 14, 1758.

George Wightman, Jr., of Warwick, and Rachel Wood, of East Greenwich, married February 11, 1759.

Thomas Remington, son of Daniel, of Warwick, and Freelove Nichols, of East Greenwich, married in East Greenwich, August 23, 1759.

William Soul and Susanna Stafford, daughter of Joseph Stafford, Jr., of East Greenwich, married in Greenwich, September 27, 1759.

Bartholomew Hunt, of North Kingstown, and Phebe Clark, of Warwick, married December 30, 1759.

John Spencer, son of Richard, and Experience Lyon, daughter of John Lyon, both of East Greenwich, married in Greenwich, February 21, 1760.

William Cowper, son of James Cowper, Jr., deceased, and Thankful Davis, daughter of Samuel Davis, both of East Greenwich, married in Greenwich, March 20, 1760.

William Hookey, son of Stephen Hookey, of Newport, and Mary Wightman, daughter of George Wightman, of North Kingstown, married in said Kingstown, April 17, 1760.

Hopkins Cook, son of Ebenezer Cook, and Annie Arnold, daughter of John Arnold, both of East Greenwich, married July 31, 1760.

Smitem Wilcox and Bethany Tallman, both of Warwick, married September 22, 1760.

Nicholas Simmons and Elizabeth Bacheldor, both of East Greenwich, married November 6, 1760.

Samuel Wightman and Amy Laton, both of East Greenwich, married December 4, 1760.

Caleb Bentley and Martha Foster, daughter of Thomas Foster, of Warwick, married June 14, 1761.

Thomas Boorman and Sarah Stafford, both of East Greenwich, married August 2, 1761.

Joseph Whitford and Desire Havens, both of Warwick, married October 9, 1761.

Thomas Stafford, of Warwick, and Rebeckah Hill, daughter of Thomas Hill, of North Kingstown, married in said Kingstown, February 4, 1762.

Thomas Tillinghast, son of Philip Tillinghast, of East Greenwich, and Mary Hill, daughter of Thomas Hill, of North Kingstown, married in said Kingstown, May 27, 1762.

Benjamin Bently and Barbara Pearce, both of East Greenwich, married November 21, 1762.

Robert Brattle, of Newport, and Susanna Pearce, of East Greenwich, married in said Greenwich, January 2, 1763.

David Corpes and Susanna Essex, both of Warwick, married February 6, 1763.

Benjamin Wood, of East Greenwich, and Margaret Price, of Warwick, married March 13, 1763.

Gideon Spencer and Phebe Burlingame, both of East Greenwich, married in East Greenwich, July 24, 1763.

John Lille and Hannah Mott, daughter of Stephen Mott, both of East Greenwich, married in Greenwich, November 24, 1763.

Henry Tibbitts, son of Henry Tibbitts, and Hannah Remington, daughter of Thomas Remington, both of Warwick, married December 15, 1763.

Fones Rice, son of Randall Rice, and Susanna Havens, daughter of Alexander Havens, deceased, both of Warwick, married February 16, 1764.

Jonathan Nillse, son of Samuel Nillse, of West Greenwich, and Avice Rice, daughter of Henry Rice, of Warwick, married February 23, 1764.

Sawdey Rouse and Hannah Sweet, both of East Greenwich, married in Warwick, April 8, 1764.

Thomas Gorton, of West Greenwich, son of Benjamin, and Susanna Pearce, daughter of Capt. John Pearce, of East Greenwich, married in Warwick, May 27, 1764.

William Warner, son of John Warner, and Waity Sweet, daughter of William Sweet, of East Greenwich, married in Warwick, July 8, 1764.

John Glaiser and Freelove Sherman, daughter of Benoni Sherman, of East Greenwich, married in said Greenwich, September 2, 1764.

William Havens, son of Alexander Havens, deceased, and Deliverance Stafford, daughter of Joseph Stafford, Jr., both of Warwick, married in Warwick, September 9, 1764.

William Wood, son of William, of Scituate, and Lydia Dowd, of Warwick, married in Greenwich, October 31, 1764.

Thomas Wilbour, son of Thomas Wilbour, of Swansey, in county of Bristol, and Mary Gorton, daughter of Samuel Gorton, *doctor*, of Warwick, married in Warwick, December 2, 1764.

Mial Salisbury, son of Martin Salisbury, of Cranston, and Ruth Greene, daughter of Deacon Thomas Greene, of Warwick, married in Warwick, December 9, 1764.

Waterman Tibbitts, son of Henry Tibbitts, and Mercy Waterterman, daughter of John Waterman, deceased, both of Warwick, married December 13, 1764.

John Bently, of Exeter, and Lucy Vaughn, of East Greenwich, married in Greenwich, April 28, 1765.

William Arnold, son of John Arnold, of East Greenwich, and Alse Wilcox, daughter of Stephen Wilcox, of Warwick, married May 2, 1765.

Jonathan Bennett, son of William, of East Greenwich, and Alse Greene, daughter of Nathaniel Greene, of Coventry, married in Warwick, May 12, 1765.

David Arnold, son of Josias Arnold, deceased, and Waity Lippitt, daughter of Moses Lippitt, both of Warwick, married in Warwick, August 29, 1765.

Stutely Wickes, son of Benjamin Wickes, deceased, and Elizabeth Greene, daughter of Deacon Thomas Greene, both of Warwick, married December 26, 1765.

Oliver Gardner, son of Isaac Gardner, of East Greenwich, deceased, and Mercy Gorton, daughter of William Gorton, of Warwick, married September 25, 1766.

Joseph Mott, son of Stephen Mott, and Martha Spencer, daughter of Thomas Spencer, both of East Greenwich, married July 7, 1768.

Richard Essex, son of Hugh Essex, of Warwick, and Mary Aylesworth, daughter of Arthur Aylesworth, of North Kingstown, married in said Kingstown, July 24, 1768.

Jeremiah Aylesworth, son of Arthur Aylesworth, and Phebe Allen, daughter of Jonathan Allen, both of North Kingstown, married in said Kingstown, July 24, 1768.

Richard Fry, son of Thomas Fry, and Sarah Arnold, daughter of John Arnold, both of East Greenwich, married in said Greenwich, August 14, 1768.

Benjamin Tifting, son of Benjamin Tifting, of Warwick, and Mary Olin, daughter of Henry Olin, of West Greenwich, married November 6, 1768.

John Allen, son of Thomas Allen, and Mary Gould, daughter of Daniel Gould, deceased, both of North Kingstown, married in said Kingstown, January 26, 1769.

William Rice, son of Thomas Rice, and Mayplet Remington, daughter of Thomas Remington, both of Warwick, married January 29, 1769.

Robert Reynolds, son of Robert Reynolds, of Exeter, and Annie Reynolds, daughter of James Reynolds, deceased, of East Greenwich, married in said Greenwich, Feb. 15, 1769.

Holden Rhodes, son of Holden Rhodes, and Susanna Wall, daughter of John Wall, both of Warwich, married March 12, 1769.

William Wood, son of William, and Ruth Gorton, daughter of Samuel Gorton, (doctor), both of Warwick, married July 5, 1769.

William Vaughn, son of George Vaughn, and Elizebeth Hackstone, daughter of Thomas Hackstone, deceased, both of East Greenwich, married in said Greenwich, December 17, 1769.

Elder James Wightman, son of John Wightman, deceased, and Susanna Eldred, daughter of William Eldred, both of East Greenwich, married in said Greenwich, January 5, 1770.

William Giles and Lydia Hazard, both of Warwick, married . June 24, 1770.

Job Pierce, son of Capt. John Pierce, and Temperance Greene, both of East Greenwich, married in said Greenwich, July 1, 1770.

Jonathan Greene, son of James Greene, of Coventry, and Lydia Nichols, daughter of Jonathan Nichols, both of East Greenwich, married in said Greenwich, October 7, 1770.

Henry Albro, son of Samuel, and Abigal Albro, daughter of John Albro, married September 29, 1771.

Stephen Greene, son of Elisha Greene, of East Greenwich, and Elizabeth Wightman, daughter of George Wightman, of North Kingstown, married in said Kingstown, December 1, 1771.

James Tripp, son of Israel Tripp, of Warwick, and Mercy Clark, of said Warwick, married in Warwick, January 30, 1772.

George Tillinghast, son of Philip Tillinghast, of East Greenwich, and Mary Greene, daughter of Job Greene, of Coventry, married in Coventry, May 28, 1772.

George Nichols, son of Jonathan Nichols, of East Greenwich, and Rachel Allen, daughter of Robert Allen, deceased, of Warwick, married August 16, 1772.

Henry Reynolds, son of Henry Reynolds, of West Greenwich, and Jemima Wightman, daughter of George Wightman, of Warwick, married September 27, 1772.

Welcome Arnold, son of Jonathan Arnold, of Smithfield, and Patience Greene, daughter of Capt. Samuel Greene, deceased, of Warwick, married February 11, 1773.

Benjamin Vaughn, son of Samuel, of East Greenwich, and Mary Bennett, daughter of William Bennett, of Warwick, married March 14, 1773.

Arthur King, and Eunice Allen, both of East Greenwich, married April 4, 1773.

William Greene, son of Rufus Greene, and Mary Sheffield, daughter of Caleb Sheffield, both of East Greenwich, married in said Greenwich, April 18, 1773.

Stephen Pierce, son of Thomas, and Lydia Rice, daughter of Peleg Rice, both of East Greenwich, married in said Greenwich, April 25, 1773.

Gideon Casey, son of Gideon Casey, and Mehitabel Baker, daughter of John Baker; of Glocester, both of Warwick, married April 25, 1773.

Thomas Fry, son of Thomas Fry, Jr., and Mary Pearce, daughter of Thomas Pearce, both of East Greenwich, in the county of Kent and colony of Rhode Island, married in said Greenwich, July 25, 1773.

Randall Rice, son of Nathan, and Rebekah Mendon, both of Warwick, married October 6, 1773.

Augustus Mumford, son of William Mumford, and Ruth Fry, daughter of John Fry, deceased, both of East Greenwich, married December 25, 1773.

Joseph Joslyn and Hope Campbell, both of East Greenwich, married in said Greenwich, January 11, 1774.

Francis Cory, son of William Cory, and Hannah Soul, daughter of Samuel Soul, both of East Greenwich, married in said Greenwich, March 27, 1774.

Nathaniel Greene, son of Nathaniel Greene, of Warwick, in the county of Kent and colony of Rhode Island, and Catherine Littlefield, daughter of John Littlefield, of New Shoreham, in the county of Newport, married July 20, 1774.

Thomas Healey, son of Joseph Healey, of East Greenwich, deceased, and Penelope Mott, daughter of Stephen Mott, married June 11, 1775.

Giles Pierce, son of Thomas Pierce, of East Greenwich, and Elizabeth Pierce, daughter of Caleb Pierce, of Warwick, deceased, married October 13, 1775.

John Singer Dexter, of Cumberland, in county of Providence, and Mary Pearce, daughter of Major Preserved Pearce, both of East Greenwich, married in said Greenwich, November 2, 1775.

Samuel Millard, of Warwick, son of Nathaniel Millard, deceased, and Sarah Jerauld, daughter of Doctor Dutee Jerauld, of Warwick, married January 29, 1776.

James Murray, of East Greenwich, and Elizabeth Scranton, daughter of Daniel Scranton, of Warwick, married February 13, 1776.

John Shaw, Jr., son of John Shaw, of East Greenwich, and Sarah Pratt, daughter of Jedediah Pratt, married August 4, 1776.

Robert Spencer, son of Caleb Spencer, of East Greenwich, and Ruth Shaw, daughter of John Shaw, married in Greenwich, September 9, 1776.

Ezra Simmons, of Swanzey, in Massachusetts, son of Bial Simmons, and Susanna Burlingame, daughter of Josias Burlingame, deceased, both of East Greenwich, married in said Greenwich, November 6, 1776.

Arnold Stafford, son of Capt. Joseph Stafford, and Phebe Sprague, daughter of Rowland Sprague, both of East Greenwich, married in Greenwich, December 2, 1766.

Samuel Pierce, son of Samuel Pierce, and Hannah Jerauld, daughter of Dutee Jerauld, both of Warwick, married December 22, 1776.

Philip Pierce, son of John Pierce, and Mary Mumford, daughter of Stephen Mumford, both of East Greenwich, married in said Greenwich, February 20, 1777.

Chandler Burlingame, son of Josias Burlingame, deceased, and Sarah Henshaw, daughter of Samuel Henshaw, deceased, both of East Greenwich, married in said Greenwich, March 26, 1777.

Benedict Arnold, son of Stephen Arnold, of Warwick, and Lydia Weaver, daughter of George Weaver, of East Greenwich, married in said Greenwich, April 6, 1777.

Thomas Rice, son of Thomas Rice, and Rosanna Blanchard, daughter of John Blanchard, deceased, both of Warwick, married April 17, 1777.

William Tallman, son of James Tallman, of Warwick, and Desire Clark, daughter of Benjamin Clark, of East Greenwich, married in said Greenwich, July 3, 1777.

William Sprague, son of Rowland Sprague, of East Greenwich, and Hannah Jenkins, married in said Greenwich, September 14, 1777.

Slade Gorton, son of Samuel Gorton, of Warwick, deceased, and Mary Whitford, daughter of George Whitford, married December 11, 1777.

John Allen, son of William Allen, of Dartmouth, Mass., and Sally Lanford, daughter of Thomas Lanford, of East Greenwich, married in said Greenwich, December 18, 1777.

Joseph Manchester, son of Matthew Manchester, of North Kingstown, and Mary Arnold, daughter of Stephen Arnold, of Warwick, married December 21, 1777.

Rejoice Bryan, son of Stephen Bryan, of Bermuda, and Asenah Spencer, daughter of Thomas Spencer, of East Greenwich, married in Greenwich, December 23, 1777.

Edward Pierce, son of John Pierce, and Waity Briggs, both of East Greenwich, married February 8, 1778.

Gorton Jerauld, son of Dr. Dutee Jerauld, and Phebe Rice, daughter of Henry Rice, both of Warwick, married February 22, 1778.

Major Samuel Ward, son of Hon. Samuel Ward, late of Westerly, deceased, and Phebe Greene, daughter of William Greene, of Warwick, married March 8, 1778.

Caleb Stutson, son of Jedediah Stutson, and Abigail Walker, daughter of John Walker, both of Warwick, married March 12, 1778.

William Searle, son of Capt. Richard Searle, of Cranston, and Catherine Greene, daughter of Capt. Benjamin Greene, of Warwick, married in said Cranston, April 23, 1778.

Jonathan Salisbury, son of Jonathan Salisbury, of Scituate, deceased, and Sarah Soul, daughter of Samuel Soul, both of East Greenwich, married in Greenwich, June 14, 1778.

Capt. Abijah Lewis, of Hopkinton, son of Nathaniel Lewis, of Charleston, deceased, and Mary Fry, widow of the late Thomas Fry, and daughter of Thomas Pierce, of East Greenwich, married June 21, 1778.

John Little, son of William Little, of South Kingstown, and Mary Pierce, daughter of Daniel Pierce, of East Greenwich, married in said Greenwich, August 8, 1778.

Joseph Arnold, son of Caleb Arnold, and Sarah Stafford, daughter of Stutely Stafford, both of Warwick, married September 6, 1778.

Christopher Weaver, son of Peleg Weaver, of East Greenwich, and Phebe Greene, daughter of Ebenezer Greene, deceased, of Warwick, married October 25, 1778.

Charles Greene, son of Rufus Greene, of East Greenwich, and Phebe Sheffield, of Warwick, daughter of Benjamin Sheffield, of Jamestown, deceased, married December 6, 1778.

Lieut. Edward Slocum, son of Ebenezer Slocum, of Tiverton, in Newport county, and Almy Lawton, daughter of Isaac Lawton, deceased, of East Greenwich, married in said Greenwich, December 30, 1778.

Lieut. Daniel Pierce, son of Thomas Pierce, and Lucy Bent⁻ley, daughter of William Bentley, both of East Greenwich, married in said Greenwich, January 10, 1779.

Solomon Wanton, of Tiverton, Newport county, and Hannah Franck, of Johnston, Providence county, married January 14, 1779.

Benjamin Franck, (Negro soldier), and Sarah Wilbour, both of Johnston, Providence county, married January 31, 1779.

Gideon Manchester, son of Matthew Manchester, of North Kingstown, and Elizabeth Levalley, daughter of Peter Levalley, of Warwick, married March 28, 1779.

Stephen Greene, son of Rufus Greene, and Patience Wall, daughter of William Wall, deceased, both of East Greenwich, married April 11, 1779.

Asahel Hooker, son of John Hooker, in the Centennial Battalion, and Almy Godfrey, daughter of John Godfrey, deceased, of East Greenwich, married April 11, 1779.

John Wilson, son of Jeremiah Wilson, deceased, of South Kingstown, Kings county, and Thankful Cooper, widow, daughter of Samuel Davis, of East Greenwich, married in said Greenwich, May 9, 1779.

Nicholas Arnold, son of Joseph Arnold, of Warwick, and Hannah Vaughn, daughter of Christopher Vaughn, of East Greenwich, married in said Greenwich, June 24, 1779.

Edward Sweeden, son of Caleb Sweeden, and Naomi Sweet, daughter of Mrs. Anna Sweet, both of East Greenwich, married October 10, 1779.

Thomas Pearce, son of Samuel Pearce, of Tolland, Conn., and Martha Jerauld, daughter of Dr. Dutee Jerauld, of Warwick, married October 10, 1779.

Philip Arnold, son of Benjamin Arnold, and Roby Gorton, daughter of Jonathan Gorton, both of Warwick, married February 3, 1780.

Rhodes Greene, son of Stephen Greene, of Warwick, and Phebe Vaughn, daughter of Christopher Vaughn, of East Greenwich, married in said Greenwich, February 6, 1780.

Benjamin Gorton, son of Dr. Samuel Gorton, and Thankful Whitford, daughter of George Whitford, both of Warwick, married March 30, 1780.

John Davis, son of William Davis, and Desire Scranton, daughter of Fones Scranton, of North Kingstown, both of East Greenwich, married in said Greenwich, June 25, 1780.

Stephen Briggs, son of George Briggs, and Huldah Gorton, daughter of Nathan Gorton, both of Warwick, married August 27, 1780.

Caleb Westcott, son of Nathan Westcott, and Susanna Greene, daughter of Caleb Greene, both of Warwick, married September 10, 1780.

John Sprague, son of Rowland Sprague, and Deliverance Pearce, daughter of Daniel Pearce, both of East Greenwich, married in said Greenwich, September 24, 1780.

Levi Peckham, son of Samuel Peckham, deceased, of Middletown, Newport county, and Sarah Tripp, daughter of Samuel Tripp, of East Greenwich, married in said Greenwich, September 24, 1780.

Joseph E. Tillinghast, son of Elisha Tillinghast, of Providence, deceased, and Miss Hermoine Brown, of East Greenwich, daughter of James Brown, of said Providence, deceased, married in Greenwich, December 5, 1780.

John Remington, son of Thomas Remington, and Mary Tillinghast, daughter of Samuel Tillinghast, both of Warwick, married December 17, 1780.

Samuel West, son of Samuel West, of Westerly, and Elizabeth Spencer, daughter of Milford Spencer, of East Greenwich, married in said Greenwich, January 17, 1781.

Thomas Westcott, son of Nathan Westcott, and Mercy Arnold, daughter of Caleb Arnold, both of Warwick, married February 4, 1781.

Thomas Foster, son of Thomas Foster, deceased, of East Greenwich, and Alse Greene, widow of the late Amos Greene, and daughter of James Tallman, of Warman, married March 18, 1781.

Samuel Allen of Pomfret, in county of Windham, in Connecticut, son of Caleb Allen, of Prudence, county of Newport, and Welthan Holden, daughter of Charles Holden, Jr., of Warwick, married April 22, 1781.

Henry Reynolds, son of Thomas Reynolds, of East Greenwich, and Millew Arnold, daughter of Mrs. Mary Arnold, of Warwick, married May 6, 1781.

Benjamin Congdon, son of Joseph Congdon, and Sarah Hawks, daughter of Thomas Hawks, both of East Greenwich, married in said Greenwich, May 10, 1781.

Prince Brown, of Coventry, (Negro), and Elizabeth Lovell, of Warwick, married October 3, 1781.

Joseph Chace, son of Abraham Chace, of Warwick, and Lucy Arnold, daughter of Oliver Arnold, of East Greenwich, married December 16, 1781.

James Greene, son of James Greene, of Nausauket, in Warwick, and Phebe Warner, daughter of Thomas Warner, deceased, married January 6, 1782.

Caleb Sprague, son of Rowland Sprague, of East Greenwich, and Lois Cassel, daughter of John Cassel, of Warwick, married in said Greenwich, February 3, 1782.

Thomas Hughes, son of Joseph Hughes, of Newport, and Welthan Greene, daughter of Col. Christopher Greene, deceased, of Warwick, married in said Warwick, February 27, 1782.

Edward Stafford, son of Stutely Stafford, of Warwick, and Almy Aldrich, of Cranston, married in said Cranston, March 21, 1782.

Olney Stone, son of John Stone, deceased, and Phebe Arnold, daughter of Simeon Arnold, both of Warwick, married April 25, 1782.

Christopher Bently, son of William Bently, and Elizabeth Mumford, daughter of Stephen Mumford, both of East Greenwich, married in Greenwich, July 14, 1782.

Samuel Rice, son of Peleg Rice, and Eleanor Pearce, daughter of Daniel Pearce, both of East Greenwich, married in Greenwich, September 1, 1782.

Jonathan Pearce, son of Daniel Pearce, and Elizabeth Coggshall, daughter of Benjamin Coggshall, both of East Greenwich, married in Greenwich, September 1, 1782.

Earle Morey, son of John Morey, of North Kingstown, and Mary Gorton, daughter of William Gorton, Jr., of Warwick, married September 1, 1782.

Hezekiah Gorton, of Voluntown, Conn., son of Joseph Gorton, of Warwick, and Mrs. Asa Potter, of Warwick, married September 12, 1782.

Joseph Gorton, son of Nathan Gorton, and Cynthia Havens, daughter of William Havens, both of Warwick, married September 15, 1782.

Henry Rice, son of Henry Rice, and Susanna Jerauld, daughter of Dr. Dutee Jerauld, both of Warwick, married September 22, 1782.

Daniel Wightman, son of Elisha Wightman, and Lydia Carpenter, daughter of Wilber Carpenter, both of Warwick, married October 6, 1782.

Thomas Warner, son of Thomas Warner, deceased, and Mary Hill, daughter of Nathaniel Hill, deceased, both of Warwick, married November 24th, 1782.

Charles Lippitt, son of Christopher Lippitt, of Cranston, deceased, and Penelope Low, daughter of Col. John Low, of Warwick, married January 12th, 1783.

Spicer Miller, son of Nathaniel Miller, and Elizabeth Fairbanks, daughter of Jonathan Fairbanks, both of Warwick, married January 30th, 1783.

Nathaniel Stone, son of Samuel Stone, of Cranston, and Mercy Gorton, daughter of William Gorton, jr., of Warwick, married March 23d, 1783.

Job Layton, son of Isaac Layton, of East Greenwich, and Barbara Johnson, daughter of Eliza Johnson, married in said Greenwich, May 15th, 1783.

James Miller, son of Nathan Miller, of Warwick, deceased, and Betsey Burlingame, daughter of William Burlingame, de-

B

ceased, of East Greenwich, married in said Greenwich, July 31st, 1783.

Peleg Weeden, son of Caleb Weeden, and Sarah Boyd, daughter of Andrew Boyd, of East Greenwich, married in said Greenwich, August 31st, 1783.

John Brushel and Darkis Fry, both of Warwick, married September 29th, 1783.

David Greene, son of Rufus Greene, of East Greenwich, and Eunice Hopkins, daughter of Jonathan Hopkins, of Middletown, in the county of Newport, married in said Middletown October 30th, 1783.

Prince Limas (Negro) and Mercy Austin, (Indian) both of East Greenwich, married in said Greenwich November 30th, 1783.

Christopher Potter, son of John Potter, and Elizabeth Baker, daughter of Oliver Baker, both of Warwick, married in said Warwick, December 14, 1783.

Pero Mowry and Margaret Spencer, (blacks) both of East Greenwich, married in Greenwich, December 28th, 1783.

Caleb Hill, son of Caleb Hill, of North Kingstown, and Sarah Greene, daughter of Thomas Greene, of Nausauket, in Warwick, married January 4th, 1784.

John Bennett, of Warwick, and Sarah Burlingame, daughter of Edmon Burlingame, deceased, of Cranston, married in Warwick, February 24, 1784.

John Weeden, son of Caleb Weeden, and Hannah Finney, daughter of Jabez Finney, both of East Greenwich, married in said Greenwich, February 29, 1784.

Samuel Gould, son of John Gould, deceased, of Newport, and Sarah Ann Campbell, daughter of Archibald Campbell, of East Greenwich, married in said Greenwich, March 28, 1784.

Edmund Arnold, son of Job Arnold, and Phebe Arnold, daughter of Philip Arnold, both of Warwick, married May 2, 1784.

Reuben Arnold, son of James Arnold, deceased, of Warwick, and Phebe Johnson, daughter of Eliza Johnson, of East Greenwich, married July 2, 1784.

Jonathan Tibbitts, son of Thomas Tibbitts, and Rebekah Tillinghast, daughter of Samuel Tillinghast, both of Warwick, married in said Warwick, July 25, 1784.

Nicholas Greene, son of Sylvester Greene, and Elizabeth Greene, daughter of Dr. James Greene, deceased, both of East Greenwich, married in said Greenwich, September 12, 1784.

Philip Arnold, son of Philip Arnold, and Dinah Rice, daughter of Olney Rice, deceased, both of Warwick, married in said Warwick, September 26, 1784.

Jonathan Andrews, son of William Andrews, of Barrington, in county of Bristol, and Susanna Miller, daughter of Nathan Miller, of Warwick, married in said Warwick, October 31, 1784.

Giles Greene, son of Giles Greene, of Warwick, and Rhoda Arnold, daughter of William Arnold, jr., married January 6th, 1785.

Daniel Carpenter, son of Wilbur Carpenter, and Phebe Wightman, daughter of Elisha Wightman, both of Warwick, married March 17th, 1785.

Joseph Carder, son of John Carder, of Warwick, deceased, and Esther Sheldon, daughter of Elder Benjamin Sheldon, of Cranston, married March 27th, 1785.

Thomas Hall, son of Abiel Hall, and Mercy Rice, daughter of Fones Rice, both of East Greenwich, married in said Greenwich, March 29th, 1785.

Silas Baker, son of Moses Baker, and Patience Brown, daughter of Joseph Brown, both of Warwick, married in said Warwick, March 31st, 1785.

Olney Baker, and Sarah Arnold, daughter of Gideon Arnold, both of Warwick, married in Warwick, April 3d, 1785.

John Joyce, son of John Joyce, deseased, and Elizabeth Remington, daughter of Thomas Remington, both of Warwick, married May 29th, 1785.

Henry Remington, son of Thomas Remington, and Margaret Levalley, daughter of Peter Levalley, both of Warwick, married September 18, 1785.

Jeremiah Bailey, son of William Bailey, of East Greenwich, and Roby Miller, daughter of Nathan Miller, of Warwick, married in Warwick, September 22, 1785.

Charles Holden, son of John Holden, of Warwick, and Mary Gorton, widow of Edward Gorton, jr., of said Warwick, deceased, daughter of Jabez Greene, of Warwick, deceased, married in Coventry, September 22, 1785.

Isaac Pierce, son of Thomas Pierce, of East Greenwich, and Sarah Vaughn, of East Greenwich, daughter of George Vaughn, of Danby, Vermont, married in Greenwich, September 27, 1785.

Benjamin Weeden, son of Caleb Weeden, deceased, and Mary Smith, daughter of John Smith, both of East Greenwich, married in Greenwich, October 2, 1785.

Richmond Springer, son of Lawrence Springer, of Tiverton, deceased, and Elizabeth Rhodes, daughter of Charles Rhodes, of Cranston, deceased, both of Warwick, married October 16, 1785.

Thomas Bennett, son of Benjamin Bennett, and Mary Garzie, daughter of Capt. John Garzie, both of East Greenwich, married in Greenwich, November 17, 1785.

William Gorton, son of Dr. Samuel Gorton, deceased, and Sarah Whitford, daughter of George Whitford, both of Warwick, married November 24, 1785.

Daniel Wicks, son of Capt. Thomas Wicks, deceased, and Sarah Whitford, daughter of George Whitford, both of Warwick, married November 24, 1785.

Dutee Weaver, and Almy Andrews, daughter of Edmund Andrews, deceased, both of East Greenwich, married in Greenwich, November 28th, 1785.

William Rice, son of Olney Rice, deceased, and Tabitha Budlong, daughter of John Budlong, both of Warwick, married December 8th, 1785.

Isaac Peckham, son of Joseph Peckham, of Middletown, county of Newport, and Ruth Tripp, daughter of Samuel Tripp, of East Greenwich, married in Greenwich, December 9, 1785.

Thomas Rice, son of Henry Rice, and Sarah Arnold, daughter of Philip Arnold, both of Warwick, married December 11, 1785.

Moses Pierce, son of Thomas Pierce, and Sarah Bentley, daughter of Benjamin Bentley, deceased, both of East Greenwich, married in Greenwich, December 25, 1785.

Samuel Sweet, son of Benjamin Sweet, deceased, and Hannah Carpenter, both of Warwick, married in said Warwick, February 2, 1786.

Christopher Andrews, son of Philip Andrews, and Freelove Rice, daughter of Job Rice, both of Warwick, married February 5th, 1786.

Sylvester Hazard, son of Dr. Robert Hazard, deceased, of South Kingstown, and Elizabeth Greene, daughter of Richard Greene, of Potowomut, in Warwick, married March 5th, 1786.

Martin Nichols, son of Robert Nichols, and Deliverance Brown, daughter of Daniel Brown, deceased, both of East Greenwich, married in Greenwich, April 2d, 1786.

Thomas Remington, son of Thomas Remington, of Warwick, deceased, and Sarah Cook, widow of Silas Cook, of Warwick, deceased, and daughter of Joseph Crawford, of Providence, deceased, both of Warwick, married May 7th, 1786.

Peleg Wightman, son of Elisha Wightman, of Cranston, and Sarah Carpenter, daughter of Wilbur Carpenter, of Warwick, married July 30, 1786.

Jonathan Potter, son of Ezra Potter, of Scituate, and Jemima Glazier, daughter of John Glazier, both of East Greenwich, married in Greenwich, August 6, 1786.

Pierce Salisbury, son of Mial Salisbury, of Cranston, and Jemima Spencer, daughter of Gideon Spencer, of Warwick, married September 2, 1786.

Gideon Wilcox, son of Smitem Wilcox, of East Greenwich, and Mary Lilly, daughter of John Lilly, married September 4th, 1786.

William Gorton, son of Benjamin Gorton, and Hannah Wightman, daughter of Philip Wightman, both of Warwick, married October 1, 1786.

William Greene, son of Benjamin Greene, and Celia Greene, daughter of William Greene, late Governor, both of Warwick, married November 7, 1786.

Anthony Arnold, son of Stephen Arnold, of Warwick, and Eunice Andrews, daughter of Jonathan Andrews, of East Greenwich, married in Greenwich, December 3, 1786.

Esek Barton, son of Stutely Barton, of Warwick, and Elizabeth Warner, daughter of Ezekiel Warner, of East Greenwich, married in Greenwich, December 6, 1786.

Anthony Arnold, alias Rice, and Ruth Arnold, daughter of William Arnold, 3d, both of Warwick, married January 4, 1787.

William Collins, son of Samuel Collins, of Warwick, deceased, and Lydia Sweet, widow, daughter of Caleb Weaden, of East

Greenwich, deceased, both of Greenwich, married in Greenwich, January 7, 1787.

Joseph Cory, son of Oliver Cory, and Esther Garzie, daughter of Capt. Garzie, both of East Greenwich, married in Greenwich, April 5, 1787.

Caleb Weaver, son of Abiel Weaver, and Freelove Gammet, daughter of Isaac Gammet, both of Warwick, married April 7, 1787.

Jonathan Austin, of Scituate, son of Pasqua Austin, of Exeter, deceased, and Mehitable Casey, widow, of Warwick, and daughter of John Baker, of Glocester, married July 22, 1787.

George Thomas, son of Samuel Thomas, of North Kingstown, deceased, and Martha Aylesworth, daughter of Philip Aylesworth, deceased, of East Greenwich, married August 19, 1787.

Samuel Brown, son of Daniel Brown, deceased, of East Greenwich, and Mary Greene, daughter of Richard Greene, deceased, of Potowonut, Warwick, married October 22, 1787.

John Coggeshall, son of Benjamin Coggeshall, of East Greenwich, and Mary Weaver, daughter of Thomas Weaver, of Newport, deceased, both of Warwick, married December 24, 1787.

William Cezer, of Providence, and Barshaby Rice, of Warwick, married in Warwick, February 3, 1788.

Lowry Church, son of William Church, and Mary Arnold, daughter of William Arnold, both of Warwick, married March 2, 1788.

Christopher Arnold, son of Stephen Arnold, of Warwick, and and Phebe Andrews, daughter of Edmund Andrews, of East Greenwich, deceased, married in Greenwich, September 18, 1788.

William Levally, son of Peter Levally, and Phebe Dexter, daughter of Benjamin Dexter, both of Warwick, married September 25, 1788.

John Arnold, son of Joseph Arnold, and Hauneritte Jerauld, daughter of James Arnold Jerauld, both of Warwick, married October 5, 1788.

Wightman Sweet, son of Benjamin Sweet, deceased, and Elizebeth Wickes, daughter of Stutely Wickes, both of Warwick, married October 12, 1788.

Pierce Reynolds, son of Shibnah Reynolds, and Anne Button, daughter of Rufus Button, of Hopkinton, both of East Greenwich, married October 15, 1788.

Daniel Tillinghast, son of Pardon Tillinghast, of Exeter, and Mary Weaver, daughter of Peleg Weaver, deceased of East Greenwich, married in Greenwich, October 26, 1788.

Andrew Boyd, and Elizebeth Spencer, widow, and daughter of William Sweet, both of East Greenwich, married in Greenwich, December 9, 1788.

Peter Sprague, son of William Sprague, of Cranston, and Mary Carpenter, daughter of Wilbour Carpenter, of Warwick, married February 19, 1789.

Clemmont Weaver, son of John Weaver, deceased, and Cynthia Spencer, daughter of Thomas Spencer, deceased, both of East Greenwich, married March 13, 1789.

James Gould, son of John Gould, of Newport, deceased, and Bethany Bently, daughter of Benjamin Bently, both of East Greenwich, married in Greenwich, March 15, 1789.

David Gorton, son of Joseph Gorton, and Elsie Whitford, daughter of George Whitford, both of Warwick, married March 19, 1789.

Richard Arnold, son of Thomas Arnold, and Honour Havens, both of Warwick, married March 19, 1789.

Stutely Stafford, son of Stutely Stafford, deceased, of Warwick, and Freelove Potter, daughter of Zuroy Potter, of Cranston, married in Cranston, March 26, 1789.

Joseph Card, son of Richard Card, and Sarah Andrews, daughter of Benoni Andrews, both of East Greenwich, married in Warwick, April 30, 1789.

John Miller, son of Nathan Miller, of Warwick, and Sarah Potter, daughter of Robert Potter, of East Greenwich, married in Greenwich, May 15, 1789.

James Tiffany, son of Thomas Tiffany, of Warwick, and Elizebeth Card, daughter of Joseph Card, of East Greenwich, married in Greenwich, May 21, 1789.

Simmons Spencer, son of John Spencer, of East Greenwich, and Amey Briggs, daughter of Joseph Briggs, of Warwick, married June 7, 1789.

Caleb Brayton, son of Francis Brayton, of Coventry, and Anne Arnold, daughter of Stephen Arnold, of Warwick, married June 25, 1789.

Pompey Mumford, and Sabin Allin, both of East Greenwich, married August 19, 1789.

Burris Lippitt, (Negro), and Mary East, daughter of William East, both of Warwick, married September 10, 1789.

Rufus Barton, son of Stutely Barton, of Warwick, and Mercy Card, daughter of Joseph Card, of East Greenwich, married in Greenwich, September 10, 1789.

Isaac Hall, son of William Hall, and Susanna Reynolds, daughter of Shibnah Reynolds, both of East Greenwich, married in Greenwich, November 22, 1789.

Anthony Rice, son of Holden Rice, deceased, and Martha Cook, daughter of Capt. Silas Cook, deceased, both of Warwick, married in Warwick, January 3, 1790.

Caleb Jerauld, son of Doctor Dutee Jerauld, and Roby Arnold, daughter of Caleb Arnold, both of Warwick, married in Warwick, January 19, 1790.

Alexander Havens, son of William Havens, and Anne Ladd, daughter of Capt. John Ladd, deceased, both of Warwick, married January 31, 1790.

Joseph Baker, son of Joseph Baker, and Sarah Wightman, daughter of Capt. Reuben Wightman, both of Warwick, married February 28, 1790.

James Levally, son of Christopher Levally, deceased, of Warwick, and Sarah Aylsworth, daughter of Richard Aylsworth, both of East Greenwich, married in Greenwich, March 15, 1790.

Samuel Stone, son of Samuel Stone, of Cranston, and Hannah Sweet, daughter of Thomas Sweet, of Warwick, married March 18, 1790.

Weeden Eldred, son of Thomas Eldred, deceased, of North Kingstown, and Mercy Comstock, daughter of Job Comstock, of East Greenwich, married in Greenwich, June 22, 1790.

Jonathan Nichols, son of Benjamin Nichols, and Mary Wightman, daughter of Philip Wightman, deceased, both of Warwick, married June 27, 1790.

John Waterman, son of William Waterman, of Warwick, and Phebe Weaver, of East Greenwich, daughter of Jonathan Weaver, married in Greenwich, July 4, 1790.

David Greene, of Warwick, and Countes Reynolds, of East Greenwich, (colored), married in Greenwich, July 18, 1790.

Benjamin Carpenter, son of Wilber Carpenter, and Mary Burk, both of Warwick, married August 29, 1790.

Harris Arnold, son of Philip Arnold, deceased, of Warwick, and Hannah Weaver, daughter of Jonathan Weaver, of East Greenwich, married in Greenwich, September 19, 1790.

Doctor Jeremiah Greene, son of Col. Christopher Greene, deceased, of Warwick, and Lydia Arnold, daughter of Colonel William Arnold, of East Greenwich, married in said Greenwich, October 7, 1790.

James Low, and Elizabeth Sambo, (Blacks), living in Warwick, married October 14, 1790.

Othniel Wightman, son of Philip Wightman, deceased, of Warwick, and Sarah Arnold, daughter of Oliver Arnold, deceased, of East Greenwich, married in Greenwich, November 4, 1790.

Abraham Pierce, and Welthan Spiwood, (Blacks), both of Warwick, married November 9, 1790.

Fones Spencer, son of Michael Spencer, and Sarah Spencer, daughter of Benjamin Spencer, deceased, both of East Greenwich, married in Greenwich, November 14, 1790.

Welcome Spencer, son of Griffin Spencer, and Mary Morris, widow, and daughter of Thomas Landford, deceased, both of East Greenwich, married March 21, 1791.

Samuel Budlong, son of Samuel Budlong, of Warwick, and Waity Salisbury, daughter of Nathan Salisbury, of Cranston, married in Cranston, April 3, 1791.

Cyrus Arnold, son of Simeon Arnold, of Warwick, and Anna Allin Potter, daughter of Zuriel Potter, of Cranston, married in said Cranston, April 14, 1791.

Elisha Wightman, Jr., son of Elisha Wightman, of Cranston, and Elizebeth Arnold, daughter of Stephen Arnold, of Warwick, married June 19, 1791.

Cato Holden, and Sarah King, both of Warwick, married in North Kingstown, July 10, 1791.

Sion Arnold, son of Oliver Arnold, deceased, and Phebe Arnold, daughter of Stephen Arnold, both of Warwick, married July 10, 1791.

David Tarbox, son of Samuel Tarbox, deceased, of East Greenwich, and Sarah Johnson, daughter of Major John Johnson, of Coventry, married in Coventry, July 17, 1791.

Samuel Remington, son of Reuel Remington, and Almy Arnold, daughter of Thomas Arnold, both of Warwick, married July 17, 1791.

Richard Burk, son of William Burk, and Mary Greene, daughter of Caleb Greene, both of Warwick, married July 17, 1791.

Lawton Spencer, son of Capt. Gideon Spencer, of Warwick, and Martha Niles, daughter of Jonathan Niles, of East Greenwich, married August 7, 1791.

Joseph Reynolds, son of Thomas Reynolds, and Sibyl Spencer, both of East Greenwich, married in Greenwich, August 8, 1791.

Wanton Rice, son of Henry Rice, and Mercy Gardner, both of Warwick, married October 2, 1791.

John Fry, son of Richard Fry, and Hannah Gorton, daughter of Mary Gorton, both of East Greenwich, married in Greenwich, October 2, 1791.

Daniel Brown, son of Clark Brown, and Margaret Briggs, daughter of Ebenezer Briggs, both of East Greenwich, married in Greenwich, October 30, 1791.

Ishmael Rhodes, of Warwick, and Martha Newfield, of Cranston, married November 20, 1791.

George Finney, son of Jabez Finney, and Hanahretty Mathews, daughter of Cobb Mathews, both of East Greenwich, married in Greenwich, May 4, 1792.